PRIMOGENESIS

Written by: **Michael J Tosner**
Illustrations by: **Michael J Tosner**

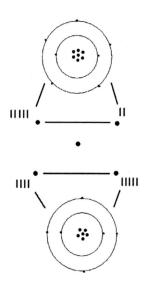

Prologue:

The tiny flame flickered, and danced along the edge of the recessed wick. Edward held his breath and recited, in his mind, the charge he'd been given;

"Keep this lantern burning!"

His numb fingers had over adjusted the wick of the oil lantern, which a moment prior had sent a sooty plume of smoke to his nostrils. Now it had shrunk too low and was flickering dangerously close to extinguished. Edward blocked the intake vents with his other hand to protect the delicate flame from the gusting wind. He stared intently at the lamp in his lap as the wick rolled slowly upward. The tiny flame began to spread again and he slowly uncovered the vent holes to allow more oxygen to the flame. It was a delicate balance of fuel and heat and air. A formula made more complex by the swirling winds on the mountain and the fragile design of the glass lantern. He was huddled now in an alcove of rock protected, for the moment, from the hardest winds and swirling snow.

No sooner had Edward found the proper wick and vent calibrations; when the ghostly image of his father's ice covered face popped into the now illuminated alcove. The melted snow and condensation from his breath had collected on his beard and eyebrows and hung an icy mask over his leathery skin.

"Let's go boy!" Frank Brein shouted over the wind, in the same hurried and serious tone he had used an hour ago to give his son the assignment;

"Keep this lantern burning!"
The low-hung three-quarter moon peered just under the cloud cover, making the task seem moot. None the less, Edward repeated his charge as he stood up and joined the rest of the motley caravan ascending the mountain.

Edward's father, Frank, slung a large sack and carried a flint lock rifle. He was under-dressed for a mountain expedition, still wearing the leather sheriff's jacket he reserved for his patrols around town. Behind them were the Ferhoff brothers each of whom carried one end of a three meter wooden ladder. They were both builders and expirienced mountanieers, and those skills were reflected in their solid frames. Bringing up the rear was the Needlin clan; Edward's schoolmate Arthur Needlin, his father Josef, and older sister Beth. Josef and Beth dragged behind them a disk shaped canvass sack, wrapped in thick iron chains. Arthur had also been designated "lantern bearer" duty, although his task was made easier by a solidly built iron lantern that was designed for outdoor use. On occasion Edward glanced back at the mysterious cargo of the Needlins, in the hope of gaining some clue to the purpose of this late night excursion.   At the moment, he only knew that his father had woken him, told him to get dressed for the mountain, and here he was: charged with keeping this oil lamp alive, as they snow-shoed their way up the glacier toward the western peaks.   The look in his father's eyes communicated a seriousness, and an urgency, Edward had never before been party to in his young life. For the first time he felt he was a part of "grown-up stuff". He did not know how to react in this environment, and so he just followed his father's orders and asked no questions.   His friend and fellow twelve year old, Arthur, bore the same look of frightened acquiescence.

Frank Brein scanned the mountain ahead as their snow shoes flopped against the wind blown glacial crust.   His son walked at his side glancing down to check the lantern with every other step.   Edward felt the sudden jolt as his feet came out from under him he felt the lamb skin parka he wore pull taunt to his armpits.   The lantern shook and Edward felt a surge of panic overcome him.   Suddenly he was eye-level with the surface of the glacier.   He looked down to see nothing but the blackness of a meter wide crevasse that disappeared into a void beneath him.   Frank Brein hoisted his son by the hood of his parka backward from the edge of the icy abyss.   The lantern flickered but remained lit as Edward sat at the edge of the crevasse.   Edwards's heart pounded through his jacket as he crawled away from the edge. Frank Brein motioned for the Ferhoff brothers who quickly hoisted the ladder across the span. Edward was shaken but could tell he was not going to receive any sympathy from this group. He had to shake it off; there was something important that needed to be done. Exactly what, he dared not ask. With great care all seven travelers crossed the wooden ladder rungs, where upon the Ferhoff brothers picked up the ladder and the caravan ventured onward. Frank had always told his son to hike the glacier with a buddy, and always be tethered to one another. This reckless late night adventure seemed to be breaking many of the protocols Edward's father had laid down over the years. This night, Frank had time for only one safety precaution for his son:

"Stay close"

Edward would do that from here on out, never getting even a single step in front of his father.

It was at the third and deepest crevasse that Frank stopped the group with a single word: "Here!".

They had nearly reached the top of the range. A hundred meters further up a giant cornice hung over the now steep slope. The cornice loomed over them, an improbable mass of snow and ice molded by the prevailing winds that blew in from the back-side bowl. Wisps of snow blew over the cornice, and sprayed more fine snow into the air turning the weather from light flurry to dense snow.

The Needlins and their mysterious chained sack came to the front of the caravan. They heaved their sack into the crevasse without delay. The long chain ends slid quickly across the snow and disappeared as if being sucked in by the crevasse. Beth and the four men peered over the edge, like pallbearers standing over a snowy grave. Thin streams of snow followed the chains into the darkness.

Arthur and Edward stood to the rear. Edward stole quick glances at the men as he maintained his lantern. After a long moment the four men seemed satisfied that the sack was gone, and turned there attention away from the dark icy pit. Beth's eyes lingered a bit longer, her stare fixed on the void. Suddenly out of the crevasse rose the canvass sack, its shackles dangling beneath it. It levitated as if by magic. Edward had heard from his teacher that there were some men experimenting with flying machines, he had even seen a print of one in the paper, but aside from kites he had never seen an inanimate object fly. Beth grabbed the dangling iron chain, and lost her balance as she was lifted and pulled over the crevasse. Josef Needlin made a hasty grab at Beth's coat but caught only her loosely tucked scarf. The scarf slid out from under her jacket with little resistance as the sack once again fell from the sky, anchored by the falling Beth.

"Beth!" Her father shouted.

Only a muffled "crack" echoed back from the bottom of the crevasse.

"Lamp boy quickly!" Frank Brein screamed to his son.

Edward approached the edge lamp outstretched and flickering in the wind.

The light exposed the mangled body of Beth Needlin at the bottom of the fifteen meter ditch. The chain wrapped around her torso, she now anchored whatever strange thing levitated beneath the canvass and iron harness. Blood soaked into the ice near Beth's head creating a large purple stain against the blue glacial ice. From the contortions of Beth's shattered spine, and the amount of blood soaking the ice around her, Frank made a quick decision that Beth was dead, or soon would be. Josef called to his daughter hoping desperately for a response.

"We have to get her" Josef cried.

The three other men shared a knowing glance.... she was lost. Frank motioned to the Ferhoffs to take care of the surviving Needlins. They quickly ushered the father and son away from the crevasse and back down the mountain. Josef continued to protest and plead for the rescue of his daughter as he struggled against the older larger Ferhoff brother. It was an awkward struggle of flopping snow shoes stumbling down the steep slope. Frank handed Edward his rifle and grabbed away from him the lantern. Edward watched in amazement as his father jumped across the crevasse and made his way up to the base of the cornice, with the sack he'd been carrying in tow.

Upon reaching the cornice he dug a small alcove in the ice wall. Three small barrels emerged from Frank's sack. Edward had seen the rail workers use those same barrels to blast away entire mountain sides, as they cleared the way for the new steam train line. Frank stacked the barrels in a pyramid and placed the lantern atop the structure. Everything placed to his liking; he stumbled back down the face. Looking down as he jumped the crevasse he noticed levitating canvass mass struggling to free itself from the chains which appeared to be loosening. He grabbed back his flintlock with one hand and Edward by the arm with the other as he yelled:

"Everyone behind that rock... get to the side!"

Everyone followed Franks lead and cut laterally across the mountain face. They gathered near a large rock protrusion, Josef Needlin being dragged as he wept for the loss of his daughter, and Arthur swept up in the arms of the younger Ferhoff brother.

"Everyone up against the rock face" Frank again commanded.

He then turned to peer around the rock wall they now hid behind. He lifted his long double barrel rifle toward the light of the lantern and took careful aim. The rifle had two barrels each paired to its own trigger and firing hammer. At the same moment the strange levitating machine was beginning to tear free from the canvass enclosure as the chains slipped around it.

Frank was no demolitions expert; he had requisitioned the black powder from the storage shed of the rail road company. He was unsure whether the impact of his bullet would be enough to set off the explosives. This black powder was a new science that, to him, was alchemy. He believed it would, but came to the realization that he would only have two shots at it. In his haste, he had not thought to bring more ammo. He only had one bullet in each chamber. He let his first shot go quickly; the thick glass base of the lantern shattered. The flame inside struggled to survive, as the chimney fell on its side and lamp oil spilled across the top of the highest barrel. The barrels, more than a hundred and fifty meters up the mountain, looked tiny to Frank. The light of the lantern was dying now making it even harder to distinguish the barrels.

In the crevasse; chains around the flying machine were inching their way down the sides of the canvass sack.

Frank's grip tightened around the rifle. The wood finish on the stock beneath his cheek bore fifty two neatly carved lines, each one a kill. Frank was a great shot and the notches he rubbed under this thumb gave a subtle reminder of that fact. Frank whispered a plea to his rifle as his finger found the second trigger.

"Come on one good shot... Just one..."
He pulled his elbows tight to his body and held a long exhale. The sights were aligned a hair below the faint flickering light, he could no longer see the barrels as he aimed at the darkness beneath the tiny spot of light. The shattered lanterns flame dropped to a faint blue before Frank could let the second shot go. He could not make his final round a shot into the dark. Frank handed the rifle to his son and grabbed the lantern from Arthur.

"Our decent just got a bit harder.. Stay here" Frank declared as he turned to bring the last of their light up the mountain.
Edward peered around the corner of the now darkened rock alcove. Watching as his father once again sprinted up the glacier toward the cornice.

Frank jumped the crevasse again catching a glimpse of the mysterious levitating sack as it began slipping through the chains that tethered it. Frank stumbled as he landed on the uphill side of the crevasse and suddenly realized that the glacier was giving out beneath him. All four of Frank's appendages clawed in a frantic scurry toward stable ice. Franks lower body dangled from the edge of the now widened crevasse. The iron lantern had landed in the snow an arms length in front of him.

As if by divine intervention the wind dropped in speed and changed direction for a moment. The tiny blue flame that had survived in the shattered glass lantern danced across the wick and found its way down to the pool of oil that capped the top powder keg.

Frank had no sooner recovered his legs from he pit when the bright blaze of fire from the cornice drew the attention of his widening pupils. Edward's eyes drew the same autonomic response as he watched from the alcove.

BOOM!

An avalanche of snow and ice stormed down the mountain. Frank was swallowed by the river of snow cascading into the crevasse. The avalanche continued until the pit was filled, and the area was capped with another meter of snow. A river of ice and snow blasted past Edward and the others as they clung tightly to the rock wall. When the rumbling quieted, and the shifting mountain had come to rest, all that could be heard was the low weeping of Josef Needlin, and the gusting wind.

Chapter I : Medicine

"Neither heaven nor hell would be this... mediocre" Zahra's inner dialogue offered as she stared at a muted green ceiling.

The dull pinch of the intravenous shunt that stung her right arm; the medical tape that pulled on the skin of her forearm, holding the shunt in place; the aching throb of the muscles around her head; the blunt pain that ran down her left leg from the knee; all of it, evidence against heaven.

The soft pillow cupping the back of her head, the smooth sheets that covered her body, the sliver of sunlight warming her forehead as it angled its way through the recovery room window; all this ruled out hell.

"No... I'm definitely still alive."

She felt as though the mattress and pillow had molded around her. How long had she been in this bed? Zahra had a sudden impulse to test her motion. She stretched her fingers, and then balled them in a weak fist. The muscles were unprepared for the task, taunt with a mild atrophy.

Zahra wiggled her toes and felt the sheets sliding across her skin. To witness the movement she tried to lift head and found her neck and shoulders creaked with pain. Her head dropped back down into the soft pillow before she could gain any meaningful perspective on her condition.

She COULD move, she knew it, but her body seemed to insist on lying still for the moment. Zahra nuzzled her head back into the pillow, tiny movements that stopped at the fringe of pain. She was alive, and she could move, and that was enough. Maybe when she awoke again the headache would be gone.

Every four hours, a small electronic box attached to the intravenous, was administering incrementally smaller doses of morphine into the drip. The LCD of the digital counter displayed zero and small droplets of the opiate crawled their way down the clear plastic tube to Zahra's arm.

Zahra saw herself twenty five years prior, as a young girl of six. The crest of the private school she attended seemed too large for her diminutive suit jacket. Her jacket and skirt cleanly pressed, and her hair tied back in a neat pony tail by thin white ribbon just above her shoulder blades. The smooth marble of the vaulted foyer at her stepfather's estate resembled an overcast sky in this vision. Her stepfather's estate always evoked a strange uncomfortable feeling in Zahra. In her dream everything was at a higher contrast. The glare from the exaggerated white of her leotards overpowered the shine of her glossy black leather shoes.

Zahra ascended the curved marble stairs into the long hallway that ported for ten bedroom doors. She walked in a trepid lurch like a child approaching some dangerous animal at a zoo. Cautiously the young Zahra slinked down the hallway to a half opened door. Pushing it wide she found her birth father, her real father, sitting naked on the edge of a king sized bed. His back was turned to the door. He was a young looking forty, with smooth skin that was a dark tan. Only the few speckles of white, in his otherwise dark and well groomed hair, betrayed his age. Zahra approached him from behind crawling up onto the bed and her father sat motionless facing the opposite direction. She walked on her knees in tiny steps across the giant bed. With a quick motion the glint of a nickel plated revolver flashed into her field of view. Attached to her fathers arm it rose like serpent about to strike at the temple of his head.

Here is where the dream always ends.

Zahra awoke to a cool breeze and the tug of the sheets moving over her body. The bed had been lowered and a thick woman with a stern face stood above her. Zahra felt the brutish nurse position her hands under her shoulder and hip. They were the strong hands of a woman who made her living lifting and moving patients. In an instant

Zahra was on her side. She now faced and elderly man whose chest was exposed under a loose hospital robe. His skin as wrinkled and muslin, as the thin disposable robe he wore. His mouth was a sad gapping over-bite, as the weakened muscles of his mandible had recessed and dropped his jaw.

By his side sat a woman in her thirties. She had the disheveled, despondent, and baggy-eyed look of a person who had been up all night waiting for death. Zahra's eyes met hers for moment until she felt a warm wet cloth sliding down her lower back and between the cheeks of her buttock. She suddenly had a keen interest in what was going on behind her. The aching pain and the tightness of her neck muscles prevented her from turning far enough to see. "Woo" Zahra tried to exclaim, but the words were lost in the raspy haze of her dry throat. She was more awake now then she'd been in nearly four days. The nurse babbled something in strange tongue that sounded like a reassurance. Something caked to her skin was peeling off under the warm rags, and she was suddenly aware of her own rancid smell. Zahra could only stare at the old man, and who she perceived to be his daughter, as the feces was cleansed from her skin.

Another smaller and younger nurse came into her view and pulled a thin privacy curtain between herself and the old man.

It had years since she had been in a hospital. She had forgotten how demoralizing an experience it was. Her left leg still throbbed with pain, as the smaller nurse lowered the bed until her abdomen was level with Zahra's head. The petite nurse cradled her head and reached under her shoulder to lift Zahra off the bed. The brutish nurse then pulled the sheets out from under her until she was lying on the plastic cover of the mattress. The young nurse had a natural blush to her cheeks and shiny black hair that framed a smooth pretty face. After a few more manipulations the two nurses had a clean set of sheets beneath her.

The young nurse lingered at the side of the bed putting a soft hand on Zahra's head brushing her hair back with her fingers. Zahra studied her face as she pushed the button that raised the bed to its normal position.

The digital counter attached to her drip again hit zero.

The nurse's long dark hair fell across her neck, and their bodies pressed against each other as she leaned over to make adjustments to the pillows. Coming back into Zahra's vision she held an ice cube, retrieved from an unseen table. The nurse held the melting cube above Zahra lips. It shimmered against the ceilings dull green backdrop. She felt a cold drop splash against

20

her esophagus, as she closed her eyes and opened her mouth in a pathetic plea. The cold drops felt sinful as they slid down her tongue and throat. All that had kept her alive for the last five days had come through the shunt in her arm. She was welcoming back this simple pleasure, a cold drink.

She smiled as she opened her eyes. The young nurse smiled back a soft smile that suggested either pride or pity, she could not tell. She retreated whispering some delicate word in what sounded like a Germanic dialect. Zahra did not understand but the message seemed to be reassurance that everything would be ok. She closed her eyes happy to be alive.

She awoke again from her recurring dream, once again staring at an uninviting green. An ex-boyfriend, and "dime store" psychologist, had insisted Zahra's reoccurring dream was "symbolic of your lack of emotional bonding with your father ", and she was "still trying to know him". He did not last long on Zahra's social calendar nor did any boy who pried too much into her past; anyone who desired intimacy.

Thoughts of her dream quickly faded to panic, as the painkillers were no longer at any meaningful dose. Zahra felt a clarity of thought she had not felt in several days. The last thing she remembered was being on the rock with her climbing guide, and friend, Andrew. Now she was in a hospital.

The pains she felt were also clearer. There was a dull pain emanating from the left side of her skull, and the pain in her leg would not cease. She gingerly lifted her hand to the left side of her head, and groped at the patch of shaven skin. Her fingers dabbed gently on the antibiotic ointment that covered the twenty stitches streaking her cranium. The patch of marred skull was starkly contrasted by the long flowing auburn hair that capped the rest of her head. Her youth and beauty afforded her much room for vanity. Her heart sank as she imagined what she must look like. Her neck was warming to idea of movement, as she scanned both sides of the bed for a call button. Finding none she called out

"Nurse!" repeatedly.

She needed to sort all this out.

She needed to get out of this place.

She would demand a doctor's council.

What she received was a priest.

"Easy Zahra" were the first words she could understand since entering the hospital. The words snuck up on her from the right side, low and regal in their tone. Zahra had not yet located their source but none the less got right to it.

"Where am I?"

Father Jolien's face appeared between Zahra and the dull green ceiling. He was a towering figure above Zahra's prone body. Guessing the young nurse to be five foot six, she put Father Jolien at six and change, even as the arch of his back was yielding to seventy years of gravity. His face, like most mountain men, appeared scorched by wind and sun. His nose was swollen and slightly disfigured from habitual sun burn. He had the appearance of an oversaturated color photo; red skin, blue eyes, slick white hair, capping a dark cassock.

"You're in the hospital." escaped in hushed tones from Jolien's mouth, as he sat down at the edge of Zahra's bed.

"Where?"

"You're in Mornel, Zahra. You had an accident, but you're alright. You're out of the woods"

Zahra felt the priest's warm hand grab hers. She had not been to church in years, and felt a tinge of guilt that quickly gave way to a sense of comfort. Zahra was already starting to remember the climb.

The events of that day shot through her mind in an instant. They approached the southeastern face. She insisted on taking the lead when they had reached a ledge near the summit. She poorly set her first two cams. The mountain streaked by as she clawed at the rock face. The first cam jerked her violently before giving way. The second cam offered less resistance. There was a third jerk on the harness that she knew now was her guide, and good friend, trying desperately to stop her fall. Falling at nearly forty miles an hour, Zahra's leg caught a crack in the rock face and felt a final violent jerk before blacking out.

"Where's Andrew?" Zahra stammered, finally pulling her friends name from her throbbing brain.

"..We buried him two days ago." He offered in his most empathetic tone.

She turned her head away from Father Jolien to contemplate this.

"Do you remember what happened up there?"

Zahra silently reran the events through her mind again.

"No" she lied.

She could sense more questions coming on the events of the hike. Explaining how her climbing incompetence had killed a man did not seem like fun.

"I need a doctor!" was her choice of diversion.

"What's the matter?" Father Jolien hushed.

"My left foot feels like it's jammed in a shoe that's three sizes too small. And my calf muscle is all cramped up."

"Your left foot?"

"Yes, now can you please get my doctor?"

Father Jolien made no move.

"I'm sorry but the doctor won't be able to help you with that."

Zahra shot the priest a dubious glare.

"Why don't we let the doctor decide that... Nurse!" Zahra protested as she started to sit up and look past the priest.

"Shhh.." Father Jolien hushed as he gently pushed her back into the bed.

"I'm certain the doctor can't help you because you have no left foot." He gently added.

"What!?"

She could feel her left foot at that very moment, and gave a labored chuckle at the absurdity of the priest's statement.

"The pains you're feeling are called phantom pains. Your brain was used to receiving signals from the nerves in your foot. Now that those nerves are gone, your brain sort of... manufactures those signals"

She sat up in a panic to verify the truth of the Jolien's statement.

Looking down the length of her body, she saw that the bulge of only one foot, her right, protruded from the sheets. She clawed at the sheets reeling them up to her chest and exposing the gauze covered stump that hung from her knee. The visual confirmation was the last Zahra needed. She slumped back down into the mattress and pillows, as if a wave had crashed down upon her.

She began to break.

Until that moment she had only been subconsciously aware of many of the horrors she had endured. The stress, the fatigue, the loneliness, and the loss she had felt over the last few days, all of it was catching up to Zahra. Father Jolien sensed the tears about to form in her eyes.

"I don't think you realize how lucky you are." Jolien whispered as he began gently rubbing the back of her clasped hand with his free one.

She was hardly listening, her mind lost in self pity.

"You could have been dead Zahra... you SHOULD have been dead."

She turned her face away from the priest.

"You should know that it's only by the grace of God that you're here. Had you not jammed your leg in that crack you probably would have met the same fate as Andrew."

"I might have preferred that!" Zahra snapped.

"I know this is a shock but I think you'll see in a few weeks that your residual limb is more than adequate to carry on a normal life."

"My 'residual limb'? What the hell is that?"

"..What's left of your leg."

Zahra felt a wave of anger come over her. She pulled her hand from the priest's delicate grasp.

"Where the fuck is my doctor? I can't believe these fucking hick doctors couldn't fix a good damn broken leg.." She ranted loudly drawing the attention of the nurses and patients around her.

"I know you're not in a good state right now... so I'll excuse your indecency; but you need some perspective. God took your leg but losing it saved you from death."

"Listen Father, I don't subscribe to the same bullshit you do!"

Father Jolien sat quietly allowing her anger to vent.

"So take the sermon to someone else. I'm sure there's a guy dieing in the next room whose been 'BLESSED' even more than me.... I've got one fucking leg now! This is supposed to be God's blessing?"

The young nurse approached the bed. She exchanged a brief word, in what Zahra recognized as the local tongue, with Father Jolien. She deciphered the word "doctor" in the exchange.

"Your doctor will stop by in few minutes to discuss the details of your rehabilitation, and tell you all about the amputation. I will tell you this much before I go; you will feel differently in a day or two... You will realize that you have been blessed. Much more so than Andrew... God loves you, and if you let him he'll help you through this."

She wanted to cry again, feeling undeserving of the sympathy and care she was receiving, but instead let her anger swell.

Father Jolien stood up to leave.

"If you want to talk about it later you just tell the nurse 'Father Jolien' and I'll stop by as soon as I can."

The Doctor explained to Zahra how she had dangled from the mountain face by her broken leg for several hours before anyone could reach her. He explained it had taken nearly twenty hours to locate, rescue and extract her from the mountain face. During those twenty hours, her left foot had not had any blood circulating through it. A bacterial infection was already setting in by the time she arrived at the hospital. Add to this her diminished ability to fight infection, and reattaching the foot was not an option. The trans-tibial amputation was the safest course. She would not be able to be fitted for a prosthetic until the swelling of the stump went down. Zahra did not intend to stay in the country long enough for that to become an issue. She would fly back home as soon as her health allowed. Once home, she would consult her personal physician before getting a prosthetic. That however would be a few days.

She spent much of those days sitting quietly in a private room that looked out over the very mountains she had lost her leg in conquest of. She had not yet talked to anyone from home, but there was no one there she wanted to talk to. There were few people that would even think twice about not hearing from her. She had been living in Mornel for three months, and before that she had spent the three months traveling. Her last call home had been to the landlord of her tiny apartment, and that had been at least a month ago. It was just a brief chat to make sure the apartment was still there, and he was receiving her checks. She had recently considered calling him again and telling him the contents of the apartment was his, and she would not be coming back. Zahra had been very close to making Mornel her home.

Zahra had a few friends that she tried to make into family. She had discovered however, that the friends she made had as little experience with what 'family' really meant as she did. They knew better than to try to keep tabs on her. Her real family was all dead, or at least dead to her. She resolved not to tell anyone about the injury until she was home. At the moment she only wanted solitude, and reflection. Being alone with her thoughts was task enough for her. She was soon taken from this chore by the Mornel police.

Sheriff Marcus Brein, head of the eleven member Mornel police force, strolled down the hospital corridor. He was thickly built, tall, and in his early forties. There was no door on Zahra's room, just privacy curtain that hung from a thin track just inside the doorway. Marcus peered through the slit of the curtain to see Zahra naked from the waist up, as she rubbed a wash cloth across her chest. A small bowl of water rested on the sliding table that wrapped under her bed. Zahra's bed was parallel to the doorway with her right side facing her observer. Her naked profile looked normal from the right. Her long auburn hair still flowed, and the smooth skin of her long right leg still poked out from the edge of the thin white sheet. Marcus noticed the barbell shaped posts that pierced both nipples of her ample breasts, and the tattoo above the right one. An ex-mistress of his had similar piercing. He used to pull and twist them until she screamed. She had run off on him two years ago. He had ignored her "safe word" one too many times. Too many times she had bled. He scared her. Marcus had a new mistress now, and he was breaking her into his sadism slowly.

In the town of Mornel surnames were institutions, and the Brein name was always synonymous with law enforcement. In a town with so little crime it was easy for a man like Marcus to be voted in on name recognition and the premise that "the apple doesn't fall far from the tree". The thinking people of Mornel recognized that in Marcus Brein's case the apple had not only fallen far, but rolled down the hill and floated down stream.

After several long moments of Marcus' lustful gawking, Zahra finally noticed her visitor through the curtain. She hastily covered herself, with the loose hospital gown. Marcus strolled out from behind the curtain as if he had just arrived, and announced himself.

"Sorry to intrude."

"Yeah you might have asked before you barged in here. Who are you?" An annoyed Zahra responded.

Marcus Brein approached the bed until the buckle of his thick black utility belt nearly touched her bicep. He put his thick hand on her shoulder, as Zahra gazed up at the towering figure.

"Listen bells.." Marcus had a tendency to assign everyone, regardless of relationship, with a nick name. It was a grade school technique that afforded him some social advantage that existed only in his own mind.

"I'm gonna ask the questions here ok. Your just sit there, look pretty, and give me the answers." He added.

"My name is Zahra"

"Yeah I know." He sneered.

Marcus pulled Zahra's passport from a satchel he carried. He began flipping through it.

"You've been getting around…. Little party girl huh?" he jabbed.

"I don't know why my travel habits are any of your business." She retorted.

"Come on Bells, you a little party girl?" he pressed as he brushed the knuckles of his open hand against her cheek.

"Get your hands off me." Zahra snapped as she slapped his hand away.

Marcus chuckled at her insubordination.

"Alright, let's talk about Andrew... How did he end up dead?"

Zahra remained silent.

"I can detain you if I have to Zahra, You're a visitor here and one of my citizens is dead. I need answers to rule out foul play." He added.

"It was an accident." Zahra snapped.

"What exactly happened?"

"I wanted to lead, be the first one up to the peak. He let me... He encouraged me." She added. Solemnly recalling the positive influence Andrew had been.

Marcus shook his head.

"You ladies always want to think your equal, but the lord never intended for you to be leading a man. You see."

Zahra could not believe that, in addition to all of the other trauma, she now had to deal with a sexist creep.

"I need you to leave, get out" she sputtered as she fought to maintain her composer.

"I'm not done with you yet Bells.." Marcus chided.

"I was at the apartment you two shared, you and Andrew. His parents have sorted out all the items that were yours, so I have them. When you are ready to collect them

32

maybe I can show you some new party girl tricks huh?" He whispered as a devious grin arched across his wide face.   Zahra covered her face and began to weep.   Marcus moved to the door seemingly satisfied with what he'd accomplished.

"Alright bells you get better so we can have some fun, alright?" He added slyly before ducking out through the curtain.

Father Jolien knew Zahra would be leaving and had been worried about her four days of quiet mourning and self pity.   Aside from his sympathy for Zahra, Father Jolien had known the climbing guide, Andrew Vokun, since he moved to Mornel fifteen years prior. He too was curious to find out exactly how such an experienced mountaineer met such an untimely end.

Jolien entered Zahra's room on the day of her departure.

"So you're going home Ms Telesco…"

Zahra sat in a wheel chair her residual leg elevated slightly, staring out at the mountains.

"Are you going to be alright?"

"I'll be fine father."

"Is there anything I can do for you?" He asked.

"Yeah as a matter of fact, I do need something." Zahra quickly responded.

"Anything, you just name it."

"Can you pick up my things from that creepy sheriff?" She asked.

"Sure. Did he say something to you?"

"He was peeking in at me as I washed myself. He kept calling me a party girl." She answered.

"Marcus Brein is a bad man, rotten from the start. " The priest nodded.

"I saw him kill an animal when he was eleven. He just left it there; killed it just for fun. He's just smart enough to know how to act around the voters here. Outsiders however are fair game to him. The less interaction you two have the better. I'll take care of getting your stuff. He knows better than to give me any guff."

"Thank you father" she sighed before returning her attention to the mountains.

The Priest also paused a moment to take in the view.

"Have you been able to reconcile your loss?"

"Reconcile?....... Is that what I have to do?"

"I think it would be a helpful thing if you were to accept that it's gone."

Zahra still had not turned to face the Priest. She sat silently by the window.

"If I might make a personal observation Zahra, and you'll have to excuse me if I seem presumptuous. I see a lot of conquest seekers come through here. Usually, like you, they come alone and they leave alone. They push themselves so hard in search of something out there..." Jolien turned his gaze to the mountain range that filled the large window. Zahra followed his eyes and turned her attentions to the mountains as well.

"What I think you need to do Zahra is look inside a little more."

"Is there a point to this?" she asked snidely.

"Well I also know you haven't found god yet, because you've told me that much. And from all this, I can only say; that you're going to need to find him."

"Alright father sign me up... what's the standard donation, you take credit cards, checks, what?"

"I don't want anything from you Zahra. I just have a lot of experience in helping people through loss, and helping people accept their mortality. You need something Zahra, something to be moving toward."

"Father, Father, please stop with the preaching!"

"Allow me one last thought; I'm a man of the cloth Zahra because I feel this a priori truth. A feeling that there is something, that there is a purpose. Now, I don't believe half the mythology and I don't place much value on all the pomp and circumstance of the religion I preach... So I don't want your money Zahra, and I don't care if you come to my church... I just know that it's a long hard road regardless of your station, and in the end there is no conquest........ no winners, or losers...... just dust.... and the lord"

"Man Alive! Does it ever stop!?" Zahra began to laugh a frustrated sarcastic laugh.

"Sorry Zahra, perhaps I am given to evangelize... I guess it's the price I pay for growing up in church."

"I wasn't aware priests could have children around here." Zahra snapped.

"No they can't. I'm just the bastard son of a cleaning woman, and the church was the only place my mother could find a helping hand. She worked whatever menial job she could find in this small town, I got dropped off at the church most mornings." Jolien stated. Zahra turned her attention again the mountains in the distance.

"I wish they'd had just made it an official crime back then.... Unwed pregnancy .... Then my mother could have served her time and been done with it. Instead being disowned, ostracized.... "

There was an awkward silence as Zahra imagined the life Father Jolien

"I've seen some adversity Zahra, and I was your age... I know what you must be going through."

Zahra offered no hint as to what it was she was feeling, so Jolien continued to probe.

"You hit thirty, and you wonder what your life is going to add up to. You just start to plan for the long term. You wonder where it's all going to....... and now this."

Father Jolien once again waited for a response.

"I guess we all get what we deserve, huh father?"

"'Deserve? That's an interesting interpretation. Is that how you feel?"

"I guess so Father." Zahra replied curtly and disinterested.

"Don't pretend that you're taking this lightly. You've been in this room staring out the window for five days. You must have been thinking about something?"

Zahra offered no response

"Why would you 'deserve' this injury Zahra?"

Zahra could feel the priests stare on the back of her head as she gazed out the window. Her mind buried a word that she could not expel, for fear of the emotions she had attached. She could not let the Priest in. The word "Devon" echoed through the chambers of her inner discourse. She could not reveal herself. She needed to fight this buried guilt. So much pain had come from that one event, that one mistake, so long ago. This Priest was stirring up uncomfortable thoughts. He was squeezing his way into Zahra's psyche. Pushing emotional buttons, and reading Zahra's fears and doubts like so many tea leaves.

Zahra turned her thoughts to the corner stone of her emotional wall; her hatred for her stepfather. The image of Zahra's stepfather shot across her mind. She could conjure him any time she needed to hate another man. He embodied the worst of humanity to her, ill tempered and gluttonous to any desire he felt.

"Tell me why you deserve this injury Zahra?"

"What the fuck do you care!" she snapped.

"Tell me why you spend a week in the hospital, yet you make no calls.... receive no visitors?" Father Jolien did not back down.

"Why can't you just let me be?" Zahra moaned.

"Tell me why you're alone right now Zahra?"

"I wish that I WERE alone, so I wouldn't have to be psycho-analyzed by some ancient priest." Zahra assailed the priest.

Father Jolien stared quietly at Zahra waiting for something.

Zahra could no longer overlay her stepfathers face on Father Jolien's. A message of genuine caring emanated from the priests eyes that forced Zahra to see him as the caring soul he was. Zahra could no longer think her way around the memories she had been avoiding. The battle to keep him out was lost.

"Devon..." Zahra whispered only half aware of who was listening.

"Who's Devon?"

"My brother." floundered through her quivering jaw.

"This could be the third..." she exhaled through her tears.

Jolien no longer wished to pry. His years in the confessional had taught him to listen now.

"When I woke up in this hospital; the first thought I can recall was wondering if I was in heaven or hell...... I-thought-I-was-dead." Zahra was contracting her words trying to get out her sentences before gasping and sobbing.

"It's been a long while since I believed in an afterlife so I didn't know why I had those thoughts....... But now I remember the last thought I had on the mountain." Zahra's voice now a low and congested.

"The mountain was rushing by me and I was clawing to stop it. I felt no resistance.. I was in a free fall.... I remember thinking... 'Please let me live' but it was not a thought, it was a prayer.... 'Please God let me live'......"

"He heard you." Father Jolien chimed.

"It's strange... that fall lasted only a second or two but I can remember a sadness as the rope gave, then I prayed to God to spare me... to forgive me....I thought of Devon .... my father ... I thought of so many things."

"Or maybe it's just that so many things are attached to that thought now?"

Zahra thought about this for a moment.

"It's ok to cry when we think about these things. One of my theology teachers told me: If your spiritually doesn't touch your every emotion, you're not doing it right." Jolien jibed.

The weight of the discussion made the simple axiom seem funny to Zahra and she gave a sniffling chuckle.

"Do you want to tell me about Devon?"

Zahra thought for moment before responding "Not right now"

Father Jolien walked over to the room's television set. On the table next to the set several video tapes were stacked in a neat pile.

"I'm sure the doctors have told you this already; but you're lucky….. Of all the limb amputations the trans-tibial is probably …."

Father Jolien struggled for a moment to find a neutral term: "the least hindering."

Shuffling the video tapes examining the labels as he continued:

"That's not to say it won't make life more difficult for you, but I think you'll find there are some amazingly functional and life-like prosthetics for this type of amputation. They'll have you walking normally in a few months."

"Everyone here's been telling me that… It doesn't seem to help me much though"

"I know several amputees. I've consoled a few in this hospital in my day, and I can tell you that life will go on…. I'm told you haven't looked at your residual limb yet?"

Zahra glanced down at the ball of gauze and medical tape that had replaced her left foot.

"These walls seem to have eyes." her tone now lighter and friendlier.

Zahra's tear ducts still welled into her sinuses but she was starting to regain her composer.

"We have a dose' on you Ms. Telesco." Father Jolien retorted with a rye smile.

"Oh boy" Zahra sniffled

"We have a rotation of priests visiting the hospital every day I'm only here every third day or so but we share information on the patients who we think need our help"

"And I haven't looked at it yet, so I must need your help?"

"It's been our experience that you won't find all you need to get through this in *'caring for you're residual limb'* or *'Prosthetic solutions for trans-tibial amputees'* " the priest offered holding up each video tape in turn.

"These doctors and nurses are great life savers. They're the best Zahra; but they're busy doing just that. They leave matters or spirit and faith to us."

"Faith healing huh father?" Zahra questioned.

"No those guys are all quacks." He responded flatly.

The priest drew a wide smile from Zahra with his quick jab at faith healing.

"Nothing I do will directly help you heal faster. But I can help you find a paradigm that will help you get through this.... It's

41

what happens in YOUR mind Zahra, ..that will make all the difference."

Zahra stared down at the dressing the nurses had so neatly applied to her wound. After a minute she leaned forward in her chair, and began unraveling the tape and gauze. Soon the swollen and stitched junction of skin that was now the end of her left leg was exposed. It was still discolored and swollen. Zahra sat upright in his chair, folding her arms and blankly staring down at her wound from the stoic pose. She still felt the phantom pains; and the disparity, between what she felt and what her eyes were telling her, generated wildly confusing thoughts in Zahra's brain. She looked at the stump as if it were some complicated trigonometric equation. She had avoided looking at the stump and when it did pass into her field of view she would tell herself it was hidden like some parlor trick. Now for the first time she was accepting that it was gone.

II: Geography

Just a mountain hamlet until some fifty years ago, the town of Mornel continued to maintain its old world charm. The exploitation of the town's recreational value had been hindered by the rugged geography. In those early days as a vacation destination, rail would only take vacationers to the town of Brig some ten kilometers and fifteen hundred vertical feet shy of the town. A single dirt road wide enough for a carriage and later motorcar provided the final link to the edge of town. Combustion engines were still not allowed into the town itself.

The 'tourists' in these early years were mostly experienced alpinists, who were willing to risk the harrowing carriage ride over icy surfaces that skirted perilous cliff faces. The result of glacial deposit from the first ice age, the entire range surrounding the town is jagged and acute, wrapping the town in a nearly closed crescent of tall peaks. It was through this tiny gap in the crescent that the single access road wound.

The highest peak of the surrounding range is unique in its abrupt pyramidal shape. In the local tongue it had been dubbed the "The Great Horn". Visible from anywhere in the town, it towers over the surrounding snow covered peaks. Too steep for snow to collect on them, the faces of the horn form a dark needle that cuts the thin blue sky.

The glaciers that flow down around the great horn and surrounding peaks, not only make for epic scenery, but also provide the town with clean drinking water. The locals were soon touting the water quality as another attraction, and mineral spas began springing up on the edges of town. As word spread of the scenic wonder, charm of the town, and the health of its waters, a cog train line was built to link the town with the outside word. The train traverses numerous gorges, and winds over through and alongside dozens of sheer rock faces, as it climbs the near two thousand vertical meters from Brig to Mornel. A cog drops from beneath the engine into sprocket in the center of the tracks, to allow the train to power its way up sections of track that the train would otherwise slide down.

In the winter season the train is packed with skiers eager to carve up the vast fields of fresh powder snow that reside above the tree line. In summer a mix of hikers and skiers would ride the rails to Mornel. The glacier offers skiing year-round, along with some wonderful guided hikes. The hikes start from town and slowly wind up the green summer mountainside, and along the glaciers edge. Expert technical climbers would flock to Mornel to test their mettle against "the great horn", as Zahra had. The spring and summer offered a breathtaking view of smooth white lifeless masses of ice abruptly ending in mossy green with speckles of lavender, pink and white alpine flowers.

A sprinkling of structures seemed anachonic, in the otherwise ancient town. One of these was the hospital on the edge of town. It featured the acute angles and curves of modern styling as well as the overtly modern indicators; like a heliport and satellite dish. Beneath the hospital lay the town morgue and coroners office.

Father Theoren Jolien always felt a bit haunted by the ceiling tracks that ran the length of the long hallway into the autopsy room. He knew that bodies were transported from the freezer rooms using metal hooks with castors that that locked into the tracks. The tracks passed right through the specially designed doors. It evoked the image of beef at a slaughter house. Jolien was accompanied by Marcus Brein. The sheriff's cold stare seemed at home in the surroundings, as the steps of the two men echoed off the hard walls and floor of the hallway.

"Good day gentlemen" medical examiner Jenna Wright greeted the two as they swung through the doors of the autopsy room.

"I didn't know you were bringing a priest Sheriff Brein?" She added with a curious note.

"Father Jolien here does the blessings for us." Marcus stated.

"How do you do?" Theoren Jolien took the opportunity to shake the new ME's hand.

"Well we haven't identified the body yet. We don't know what religion she is, or if she'd want a Prie.."

"Peaches!" Marcus interupted, and stepped closer to Jenna. He dropped his voice as he continued: "I think it's nice that we have a female M.E. now, believe me you're much nicer on the eyes than old doc Letham. But let me tell you how it works here; I'm the sheriff, and if you die in my town you get a priest, or you get nothing... Understand? I don't go for all that P.C. bullshit." Marcus added.

Jenna was held speechless by the sheriff's truculent tone. A tone made surreal by the fact that they emanated from a man she knew to be a moron.

Father Jolien noticed her discomfort and sensed the anger building in the young doctor. "I just say a few words, pretty nondenominational stuff." He offered grabbing Jenna's arm and ushering her away from Marcus Brein. Jenna read the empathetic expression on Father Jolien's face as meaning "don't waste your energy". She followed his nonverbal advice; guiding Father Jolien across the room to gurney covered with a thin white sheet. Marcus followed closely behind.

Jenna pulled the thin veil from the gurney exposing the ghostly, grey, and half-thawed body of Beth Needlin. Her appendages where bent in impossible contortions. Her body lay on its side, folded on itself at the waist. Her heels touched the back of her head, and her arms were twisted in opposite directions around her body. Nearly eighty years of pressure had also flattened and stretched the body into a grotesque abstract form. Beth's golden hair had already defrosted into a frizzy splash of color on the otherwise livid mass.

"What do you know about her so far?" Father Jolien inquired.

"Well she was around sixteen when she died... All of her clothes are hand made; her coat, her pants. Sewn to the inside of her pocket was a length of yarn and attached to that was a skeleton key. Cursory examination of her teeth showed one pulled tooth and several small cavities but no modern dental work. Based on all that, my first guess on time of death would be about seventy or eighty years ago..... We also found a wooden frame snow shoe and a rusted iron chain that was loosely wrapped around her body." Jenna offered as she pulled surgical gloves over her dainty hands.

"She was found on the moraine when the snow melted back. Looks like she was bound and dumped up there." Marcus quickly surmised.

"Actually, no." Jenna scoffed "There are no ligature marks on her wrists or ankles."

"Maybe she was bound around the waist or neck." Marcus returned in the same tone.

"Nope nothing there either." Jenna stated with less interest in provoking Marcus than in staying focused on facts.

"One strange thing on her abdomen though." Jenna continued as she peeled moist layers of clothing from Beth's softening body. The two men stepped around the gurney to peer over Jenna's shoulder at the marks on Beth's stomach; a large round welt centering a two oval shaped undulated pedals of scar tissue.

"Almost looks like a bow tie." Father Jolien noted.

"Is that some kind of brand?" Marcus wondered aloud.

"The lines appear to be burn marks, but there is no depression in the skin, like you'd see if a hot object were pressed into the skin. It is similar to the type of burns we see in electrocutions." Jenna explained.

"But you said the body appeared to be seventy to eighty years old, did the town have electricity then?" Jolien questioned.

"No, they didn't.. That would be the strange part.. But we'll know more once she fully thaws. Then we can straighten her out for an MRI." Jenna submitted.

The radio on Marcus's belt let out a squelch before the voice of deputy Weiss filtered though a layer of static.

"Marcus, you there?"

Marcus lifted the boxy radio to his mouth and replied:

"Yeah go ahead."

"I got someone here at the station; he says he's come to claim the body."

"I'll be right up." Marcus declared before holstering his radio.

"Well it looks like we may not have to wait so long, for those answers." Marcus sneered in the direction of Jenna, before turning to exit the morgue.

Once the swinging doors had come to rest behind Marcus, Jenna let out a groan before unloading on Father Jolien:

"I can not believe what an asshole that.. excuse me father... what a jerk that man is." Jenna exhaled.

"That's ok, I've heard plenty worse... That asshole thinks he's going to be mayor one day." Theoren joked.

"God help us." Jenna quipped.

Zahra's train schedule showed she would pull into Mornel at 8:24. "Another two hour train ride" she thought. The sun had only begun to peek over the range surrounding the tiny industrial town of Brig. Zahra stood alone on the low platform looking down the train tracks that seemed to fade into the morning mist. This leg of her journey would be on the "cog train" designed to climb to the highest elevations.

It had a large sprocket that dropped from under the engine's center. The sprockets would marry the thick iron teeth that centered the rails on the steepest inclines. Based on the cultural emphasis placed on precision and engineering she was sure the conductor would have her there exactly on time. She glanced at her watch, then the train schedule. The train was scheduled to depart brig in two minutes. She glanced again down the fading tracks toward the misty train yard, as a boxy orange mass emerged.

"Right on time" she whispered to herself. The old priest was expecting her on the 11:26, so she would have several hours to kill in Mornel before their rendezvous.

She claimed a section of four seats facing each other. Her backpack spread across two of the seats and her body loosely arranged across the other two. She leaned her head against the window, and watched as a few scant passengers appeared out of mist from the general direction of the ticketing station.

Only a bearded man in his fifties entered her car. He carried what she surmised were skis, and a large green duffle bag. He stowed his gear in the large booth designed for oversized luggage at the front of the car, then took a seat several rows in front of Zahra, facing forward, as she did.

It had been a clear day the first time Zahra found herself in Brig....

three years ago now.

She recalled being woken up by a surly conductor yelling at her in language she did not understand. Her head ached like she had been whacked with a shovel. Her vision so burly... maybe it was two conductors. She awoke again three hours later leaned against an iron stanchion on the train platform. She had stumbled to a convenient berth between two vending machines. She smelt like vomit and the heavy backpack that rested on her thighs had cut off the circulation to her legs. She rolled the bag off her as she fell to her side and began massaging the "pins and needles" feeling form her leg.

Zahra's smirk reflected back at her in the clean glass of the train window, as she recalled this detail. "An omen perhaps?"

She recalled the bright afternoon sun stinging her eyes as she tried to figure out where she was. She could not, at that time, even recall where she was headed. She forced her eyes to adjust even as her brain ached from the visual stimulation. She looked up at the beautiful snow capped mountains that surrounded Brig, defined crisply by the deep blue sky. Mountains that dwarfed the man made structures at their feet. Three large black birds seemed to dance in the center of the blue canvass she stared up at. "How long had it been now? ..... three hundred days" she wondered. She had been bouncing around the hemisphere from one party zone to the next. She recalled bragging to man she would later take back to her hotel that she had been to fifty two cities. That had to be three weeks ago; she struggled to remember where she'd been since then. The alcohol and drugs were taking a toll on her memory. She tugged at her vomit stained blouse to investigate a stinging sensation above her left breast. She found a fresh tattoo of a symbol she did not recognize stenciled into her skin. She felt nothing, and cared little at the moment for deciphering the symbols meaning.

Again she turned her attention to the mountains. The cog train pulled out of the station and began its climb, "Mornel" read a placard on its side. "Perhaps the next party city is not where I should be headed" Zahra began to reason. Maybe there was something up there. Maybe she would find something in the mountains. These were her thoughts on that clear day three years prior.

Zahra remembered that day with a certain reverence. It was a turning point, a crossroad, perhaps "the crossroad" of her life. The Zahra of three years prior found herself on the next train to Mornel, and here she was again headed for that sleepy alpine town.   The train lurched into motion, as Zahra's mind lingered on the events of her life that had taken her to that crossroad.

Her mind took her back four and a half years.   Her step father had just died leaving her a large chuck of money by normal standards, but a pittance by his. Her step brother would be the heir to his fortune. It was nearly surreal how she had found out about his demise.

Zahra was working as a life guard. It was a gorgeous day, and she had lucked into the choice assignment of the kiddy pool watch. Just four small kids in the pool, all of them attached to their mothers.   Zahra was still hung over from the previous night's debauchery, most of which she only vaguely remembered.   She had her eyes closed beneath her dark sunglasses enjoying the warm sun on her skin, when she felt a tap on her shoulder.

"You.. Zay-ra Teli-sko??" greeted Zahra as she glanced down at weasely looking mustached fellow. He wore a thin grey suit that wavered even in the gentle breeze. It was well worn and spotted with coffee and grease stains.

"Yeah…"   She noticed the large blue envelope in his hand before she continued.
"That's me."   Thinking for a moment that the interaction reminded her of how dead beat dads got served court papers. Had the previous night been THAT rowdy?

"You gotta sign for this." emanated from under the black bush of his upper lip. He raised a clipboard and pen toward her.

She added an illegible scrawl to the document intentionally missing the line that had been highlighted and X'ed for her, before dropping the clipboard to the ground. She grabbed the envelope from the man as he bent down to retrieve his clipboard.

He gave a sarcastic "Thanks" inspecting the apathetic signature, then turning to leave.

Zahra slid a stack of papers out of the envelope. Attached to the top document a simple hand written note:

> **"Dad's dead.   If you want your money send me back these forms. Tommy"**

He was 'dad' to Tommy, …. 'the prick' to her.

She felt nothing.

A month later she retrieved her bank statement, from the broken unlocked aluminum box that served as the mail drop for her apartment.   She climbed the three floors to the dilapidated studio she called home.   She sat down at the wobbly table she had salvaged from the curb, and contemplated her Spartan existence.   Staring at the balance, she thought for a moment about buying a house with her new found wealth.   Upon further consideration she did not want to be reminded everyday of 'the prick' and his money.   She decided she would not spend his money on anything she would keep.   She would blast the money away, on what she hoped would be enough good memories to wash away the four years of horror she had endured under his rule.

What followed was a haze of alcohol, sex and drugs she did not care to recollect. When she thought about it now, other that hurting her step father, she could not find a motive for her actions.   "The prick" would have disapproved of her actions, but he was also already dead.   She choose now to focus on the fact that she had awoken, on that cool clear day, to a truth she still struggled to define.

The cog train approached a steep incline, and the thick iron teeth began to rattle against the center sprockets of the track.   Zahra thought of all these memories on the train to Mornel. New thoughts, new images seemed to flash through her mind with each "clack" of the cog trains teeth.

Zahra strolled the thin mercantile canyon that was Mornel's main street; her backpack in tow. Zahra decided to get a bite to eat then do some of the grocery shopping to stock the tiny Chalet she had rented. Zahra was dealing with some "phantom pains" that pulsating from her nonexistent foot. She knew it was from sitting too long on the plane and trains, and not stimulating the stump enough. The nerve cells, that for so many years produced fired and processed neurons up the neural pathway from her leg, wanted to remain active. If the stump was not stimulated enough these cells would release a firestorm of neurons that created the phantom pains.

At home Zahra had a vibrating massager she used mostly to stimulate her stump... Mostly. In packing she had forgotten to take it from her bedside table. She would need to find a suitable replacement before heading back on another twelve hour plane ride.

On her first adventure to Mornel, "Reistling's Tavern" had provided Zahra with her first good meal, and thus held a special place in her recollection of the town. As the town sprung up from tiny hamlet to large vacation town a small group of original settlers held onto their lands. Five families owned a large portion of the businesses and hotels. Inter-marriage, between this small group of families, created a conglomerate of interwoven relations in the Mornel population. The end result was that 70% of the town was owned a group of relatives. They would later pass a town ordinance forbidding the purchase of land by anyone who was not born in the town. Everywhere in town the names Jolien, Turner, Farhoff, Reisling, and Needlin adorned bars and hotels and stores.

Reistling's tavern was an interesting and asymmetric building. The main entrance facing the street was three stories tall on the left and two stories on the right. A single-plane slate roof sloped sharply down to the right. The joists that supported the second floor cantilevered out of the building's left face and supported a large deck. Under the deck an alleyway ran down a slight incline to a small chapel, then continued down to the town's original graveyard. In the afternoon, après skiers, and hikers would fill the deck, and their boisterous tales of the day's adventure would echo from the surrounding buildings. To Zahra the deck had always seemed uncomfortably quiet in the morning, as the pendants of beer and liquor vendors dangled from its banister.

The interior was a showcase of exposed wooden beams, planks and joists, thinly lacquered to maintain a rustic look and feel. It was also a popular place for the locals to meet, most of whom appeared as rustic as the fixtures, which enhanced the ambiance. Zahra spotted a lone patron sipping some hot beverage in a window booth. There were no floor waitresses to be found. Only the barmaid, Verna Reistling, worked the bar apparently occupied with the inventory of bottles.

Three years prior she had met Verna, and decided to make it easy on her by taking a stool close to her at the bar. Verna was a portly, gap toothed, and haggard woman, who swigged her own little bottle intermittently as she served. She showed a hint of recognition as she passed Zahra a menu, then pointed a meaty finger at her as if to ask her name. Upon hearing it, she asked it she was the same Zahra Telesco that "had the accident them years back?".

She had put away most of her pride but a part of her was still stung by the thought of the locals referring to her as "the idiot who nearly killed herself climbing the horn". As she was sure the locals chuckled over the misfortunes of any weekend warrior who tried to summit the great horn and failed. They had a sort of local "mountain man" pride they liked to hold over the tourists. She chalked it up as schadenfreude that stemmed from the feeling of servitude inherent to a service and tourism economy.

Zahra was sure the idle conversation that followed was a recording of the last exchange she'd had with her three years ago, and had been looped to a hundred other tourists as well. She was also sure that few memories eddied long, in the steady current of alcohol Verna poured through her brain. Regardless of her poor state, her decades of bar tending experience had her on auto-pilot. Almost reflexively she inquired about Zahra's vacation itinerary and feigned interest in her personal, and professional life, and gave the same performance, she'd given her four times before. She mentioned in the discussion that the summer had been unusually warm and that the glacier was receded back further than she had ever seen it. She mentioned that the melt water from the glacier was causing some muddy conditions on a lot of the lower hiking trails, and the glacier skiing was "slushy" after eleven am. Zahra assumed Verna had heard these things from patrons, as she looked as if she'd not been sober enough to ski or hike in a decade. That was about the extent of the useful information derived from Verna, as Zahra leisurely ate her breakfast.

Zahra would make one stop at the "large", by Mornel standards, supper market/department store, before catching a cab to the chalet. Zahra found all of the food items she required there. She had even been pleasantly surprised to find a "personal massager" amongst the selection of pharmaceuticals the store stocked.

Zahra's "cab" was a light blue box of aluminum and Plexiglas, built small and light to require the power of only a tiny electric engine. The perfect rectangular shape reminded Zahra of the tiny wooden cars she played with as a child. Even after spending four months in the town three years ago, she was still in awe of its scenic wonder and old world charm. Some structures appeared so old to Zahra that she felt as if they had been recently unearthed for her examination. She was glad the tiny electric cab moved slowly, as she studied each of the ancient buildings with keen interest. Zahra heard nothing outside over the faint hum of the cabs electric motor. It was a refreshing change from the noise of her normal urban existence. Zahra recognized the chalet she had rented as the cab bounced its way up the thin dirt road.

Just two hundred meters up the mountain, and in stark contrast to her ancient housing, was the villa of physicist Bernard Heisten. He was famous in the manner scientists can be; that is to say accomplished but unknown outside the scientific community. A native of Mornel, he had chosen to live out his final years in the mountains, by building himself an energy efficient, "space aged" house. The house had solar panels for its electrical needs and a geothermal heat pump for heating. The heat pump ran water down to a closed loop of pipe that was buried 15 feet below the surface of the property. The bedrock deep below the surface maintained a constant twenty degrees Celsius. The warm water that was retuned from the bedrock was then pumped throughout the house. The simplicity and efficiency was quite amazing. Zahra remembered hearing the locals complaining about Bernard's house when he was finishing its construction three years ago. She recalled the main complaint of the town's people was its ultra-modern design. It did not help that Bernard failed to attend Father Jolien's weekly service, and failed to engage in the local politics. Zahra however admired the villas bold angles and flowing design. She was pleasantly surprised to find it in such close proximity to her accommodations.

The Glacier was Mornel's life blood. When it became undeniable truth that its shrinkage was due to global warming, Bernard's energy efficient house took on a new light. Though the energy consumption of the small mountain town had little impact in the grand scheme of things, the town's people made it a matter of civic pride to set the example for the world. Before long, the streetlights in town are shut off after 11pm, and solar panels showed up on the roof of every modern building. The oldest buildings were left untouched on the exterior to maintain the towns charm but wherever possible the interiors were overhauled for energy efficiency. Light switches that turn themselves off after fifteen minutes were installed, and old plaster walls had insulation blown in. Geothermal heating systems became the norm with new construction. On the back side of the mountains, to the west of town, a wind and solar power farm was built. The town cut its electrical consumption down so much that eighty percent of the towns power was now provided by these wind generators.

Zahra was to meet Father Jolien at the chalet, which was actually a three hundred year old feed storage house. The interior was remodeled and a septic system had been installed. These quaint accommodations are no cheaper than some of the finer hotels in town, and are actually quite fashionable because of their unique architecture, and rustic charm. These "old world" feed houses rest on a foundation of wooden beams that are truncated by thick stone disks. The stone disks interrupt the foundation posts about three feet off the ground, and serve to prevent rodents from climbing up into the feed house. The bulk of the feed house was then built on top of these stone disks. The roof was fashioned from overlapping stone slabs. The living space inside was a single open space about ten meters squared. There was a tiny kitchenette area to the left as one entered, and to the right was a couch and small coffee table. Centering this open space was a cast iron wood stove, the houses only source of heat. Electricity had been run to the chalet to power a small water heater, refrigerator, and electric cooking stove. Two beds were in the loft that hung over the rear half of the house. A thick wooden ladder provided the only access to the sleeping area. The quaint and rustic accommodations were situated "slope side" overlooking the town from its eastern perimeter.

Zahra put away the perishables she had purchased, but left the dry goods in the paper shopping bag on the table. She removed the personal massager from the bag and tested it briefly against her thigh, before throwing it up onto the loft bed. It was harder and smoother than the one she was used to, but it would do the job. Her dietary and personal needs attended to, Zahra turned her attention to taking the chill from the chalet by firing up the wood stove.

An hour and a half after arriving, Zahra had "settled in" and emerged from the tiny chalet that now plumed a string of grey smoke. In her hand she clenched a thick black sketch book and an array of pencils. She quickly found a large rock outside the chalet and sat down to sketch until Father Jolien arrived. Zahra loved exploring her creative talents in her free time, and was most fond of sketching. Even though she was not a very good artist, she had come to find the exercise both soothing and rewarding.

III: Spiritual beings

Father Jolien slowly ascended up the thin road toward Zahra. The cassock he wore was different from the one she remembered from the hospital. It was shorter in length, the material thicker, and a thick set of brown hiking boots now strode out from under the hem.

"Don't you believe in cabs?" Zahra called down the road to him, as she put down her sketching utensils and began closing the gap between them.

"Got to keep moving or the devil might catch me." Jolien chuckled.

Zahra greeted the old Priest with a gentle hug.

"You can hug tighter than that. I'm not going to break." Jolien stated as he tightened his arms around Zahra, and she responded in kind.

"So this is your room for the week?" Jolien said motioning to the tiny chalet.

"Yeah, just the bare necessities." Zahra chimed.

"I was in this building as a child, when it was the Reisling's feed house. I have not been in since." Jolien noted with a hint of wonder.

"Let me give you the tour then."

Each wall of the chalet had but one small window, but the bright white

68

reflections coming off the surrounding snow capped mountains bounced in from all angles. The stark light caught the dust particles that seemed to forever linger in the air of the old barn. Jolien appeared at home amongst the old timber interior of the feed house, while Zahra's smooth skin and shinny synthetic hiking apparel clashed with the well worn surroundings. He took a quick loop around the small room before commenting:

"The only amenity this little barn had sixty years ago was a pile of hay."

She smiled at thought of young Father Jolien in the old feed house.

"Can I make you some tea?" Zahra asked

"Sure.... I'm glad you wrote me" Jolien began. "I'm glad you came back"

She held her hand over the burner until the hot air signaled its proper function, then took a deep breath knowing she had planned to exorcize some inner demons with the Priest.

"I was glad when you wrote that you did not seem to be focused on proving something." Jolien continued. "It would be a mistake to try to take on the summit"

"No..... Just going to explore a little. ... inside and out." Zahra replied softly.

"Maybe feel whole again."

"Well this is a good place for that." Father Jolien smiled.

Zahra sat down across form the Priest.

"You look great.. I hardly notice any limp." Jolien noted.

"Yeah I'm doing alright with it. It feels almost natural now. I don't think about it much anymore as I'm moving around."

"That's good….." Jolien pause before turning to the heart of the matter he was there to address: "How are you doing with the internal stuff?"

Zahra was silent.

"I recall when we spoke three years ago you mentioned your brother, and mumbled that the accident with Andrew could be your third?... do you want to talk about that now?"

Zahra seemed to be gathering herself. The Priest waited patiently for a response.

"I mentioned Devon. He was fourteen months" She finally exhaled. "I was eleven and my father asked me to watch him as he worked in the yard…. My mother was out.. I don't know where…. she always seemed to be out. I think she was cheating on my father. Though, I'll never get that admission from her."

Jolien nodded and pursed his lips in silent recognition.

"He was in the play pen and I was watching TV…. And ah…" Zahra fought to continue as the priest scooted his chair around the table next to Zahra. "I didn't notice him stand up and grab the box of tissues from the table next to the pen." Zahra was tearing now.

"He started eating the tissues and began choking. But I couldn't hear it over the TV."
A pained expression flashed across Zahra's face, that she quickly pulled back.
The priest again waited as Zahra gathered herself.

"Dad came in screaming, and grabbed him up....... He was this ashy blue color.... Lifeless......"
Jolien put his arm around Zahra and pulled her closer to him as she continued now weeping openly.

"He kind'a flung him onto the dinning room table.... He was limp... tried to do CPR......." She sobbed
Jolien pulled her head to his chest.

"He was gone.."
Jolien arms wrapped tighter around her.

"It's ok these things happen, it's not your fault." He whispered as he stroked her back.

"I should have been watching.. It all would have been different."

"You were ELEVEN .... Just a kid Zahra... It's not your fault." The priest assured.
Zahra wiped her eyes with her hands as the priest dug in his cassock for his handkerchief.

"Does your father blame you?"

"He disappeared.... He could not even look at me in the months after the accident, then he just left.... I never heard from him again."

The priest furrowed his brow, bewildered at the actions of her father.

"I can't blame him when I look back. My Mother was a hand full. They were shaky to begin with, then loosing the son he wanted so badly...."

This was the juncture of Zahra's telling of her sad life story, where she would usually stop. The years with her step father too dark to share. As the priest silently processed the baggage Zahra had been carrying, Zahra thought about how far she would let him in. She committed in those silent moments to go all the way to the core, the dark heart of her neurosis, if the priest pushed her there.

Zahra braced herself for the follow up questions that would lead to that dark place.

The questions never came.

Father Jolien only hugged her, stroked her hair, and whispered repeatedly that everything would be alright.

Marcus Brein climbed the circular stair case to the glass enclosed lookout station. The guard post was intentionally dark. Tiny florescent lights focused light downward onto the consoles, but the rest of the room was shadow; save for the glint of what little light there was bouncing off Brein's gold badge.

The lone guardsmen addressed Marcus without turning his head from the console.

"They still playing?"

"Three to two.. us." Marcus replied as he tossed a thick envelope onto the keyboard.

"I don't have to count this?" The guards asked sneaking a quick peek at the stack of bills inside.

"No.... It's all there.. That junior, 'Klien', scored the go-ahead..... Can't you see it from here?"

"Church steeple blocks the view." The guard responded.

Marcus picked up a tall set of binoculars that rested on the window ledge and confirmed the guard's statement.

"Heard the glacier spit out a body... Anyone we know?" the guard grinned.

"No some broad got buried in the glacier, they think eighty years ago. I had nothing to do with it... You think I'm that sloppy?" Marcus jibed still focusing the binoculars.

"That crazy old coot Arthur Needlin came in to claim it was his sister." Marcus continued.

"No real leads then?"

"No, we've arrested him three times for accosting people. He seems to have it in for Dr Heisten..... vandalized his place when it was first built.... Anyway, we have no record of his sister, and his son doesn't remember hearing about any aunt."

"You could just run a DNA test." the guardsmen offered.

"Yeah we already have that going."

"There they are" The guardsmen declared as he tapped on the computer screen in front of him.

Marcus peered over the guard's shoulder at the infrared image of six men descending the mountain. . The source of the image was the high resolution infrared camera, trained on the towns eastern range from their guard post located halfway up the slope of the western range. The eastern range formed a natural political boundary. The outpost was installed to monitor drug smuggling traffic, which came mostly form one direction, into Mornel. During daylight hours they relied on visual surveillance from outposts near the peaks of the eastern range. During the night they turned on the infrared monitoring system to detect any activity above the tree line. Computers scanned the infrared images for any living thing that moved in the direction of the peaks, filtering out those images that matched known wildlife.

"It's not recording?"

"No the system is turned off. There will be no record." The guardsmen declared

"Good"

"So who are these guys come'n over, or is better I don't know?"

"Well the pansy ass liberals like to exaggerate things, call them war criminals. I call them good soldiers of the lord. Hunted like dogs for years, just for doing his work, exterminating vermin." Marcus hissed.

"Alright, maybe I don't want to know." The guardsmen interjected to cut off a brewing tirade.

"I'm starting to think you're not really on our side here. Do I have to worry about you?" Marcus added as he placed a threatening grip on the guards shoulder.

"As long as the money is there, you don't have to worry about a thing." He responded coldly, as Marcus stared back at him waiting for further assurance.

"I just am not as riled up on the whole master race thing as you are." He assured Marcus.

Marcus shook his head in disappointment before turning his attention to the infrared images on the tiny screen. He watched for a moment longer before taking his leave.

"Alright, seems we're all set here. I have a rendezvous to make. I'll let you know when I have more business for you." Marcus stated as he began his decent from the tower.

"Will do Marcus….. pleasure doing business with you."

In the quiet of a country morning one realizes the effect of city noise on sleep. Waking up in dead silence and clean air

Zahra felt more rested than she'd felt in a long while. There had been no garbage truck rumbling by at 3am, no cars honking. She noted these differences as she sat on the edge of the bed and rubbed the crust from her eyes. It was probably around 10:30 by the time she had gotten out of bed. She took a moment to appreciate the change of scenery she found herself in, before reaching for her prosthetic as it leaned against the side of the bed.

Zahra inspected her residual limb. It was tight and callous now, far different from the swollen pulpy stump she first inspected three years prior. Her prosthetic slid snuggly over her stump. She would always pause a for second to admire the mechanics of it.

Zahra made her way slowly down the wooden ladder that accessed the loft. It was not an altogether simple task in the haze of her waking moments, even if she'd had two good legs.

The iron stove had kept the room fairly warm through the night, and there was still a faint glow poking out from under the blanket of ash that covered the bottom of the stove. She opened the iron door, and placed some kindling on the embers. With a gentle breath she blew the ash from the top of the embers. Another gentle breath was all that was needed to ignite the kindling. A single log would take the morning chill out of the chalet. The afternoon sun would maintain the warmth until the evening. A small electric stove sat next to the refrigerator. The chalet was stocked with utensils, plates, and other basic household supplies. There would be no maid or room service. The chalet was equipped with durability in mind, as the plates and other house ware items were made from strong pliable plastic. All the cookware was heavy iron, well worn and seasoned.

Zahra cracked two eggs against the edge of a thick iron frying pan. Her lifestyle had not required her to cook for herself much. Although she had learned to cook over the prior two years, she had never acquired the love for cooking one needs to be any good at it. She was inclined to pass on cooking when any excuse presented itself. It seemed the mountain was already challenging her to be more self reliant. She smiled at the idea, as she scrambled her eggs.

A stop at the sporting goods store would be needed before she undertook any hike. Her quick inventory of what she needed included; crampons in case she hiked the glacier, a water bladder for her pack, and elevation maps.

Zahra was not a morning person and absolutely required a shower to wakeup. She would also need to restock the log rack with new wood for that evening's fire. These items were appended to the itinerary in her head as she as she leaned against the now idle stove eating her eggs from the iron pan.

Zahra had no sooner stepped out the door to perform her wood collecting chore when she heard the rusting of paper growing louder in her ear. As she turned to look she was struck in the head by a light but fast moving object. The shock of the unexpected jarring of her head caused Zahra to fall and take cover. The impact was enough to cause a small cut on her forehead. Opening her eyes, she found that her assailant was a small wood and paper kite.

Her eyes followed the bright yellow string to find a young girl running toward her. The girl was followed closely by a slight and bald headed man with a silvery grey goatee. The elderly man appeared to be in his seventies, but in good shape as he jogged briskly to catch the child. The child scurried up to Zahra and reached for the kite that was lying at her feet. She picked it up gently as if it were an injured bird, and looked at Zahra with disappointment in her eyes and lips. Zahra smiled down at her in an attempt to lighten her mood when the elderly man called out:

"So sorry madam! Kite got away a bit there. Are you alright?"

"I'm fine" Zahra replied in a conversational tone once the stranger had drawn close enough.

"Your child here seems a little scared of me?"

"That is my grand daughter Heidi. She's just a little shy. Heidi, can you tell the nice woman that we are sorry for whacking her on the head?"

"sawry" the child managed to press out as she took her uncles hand.

"Bernard Heisten." He said offering his free hand.

Zahra was shocked that she had not recognized the great physicist as he approached. Dr. Heisten's dark thick eyebrows, contrasted both his smooth round head and neatly trimmed silver goatee. Bernard caught the look of recognition that that was sweeping across Zahra's face, and answered her next question before she could ask it.

"Yes that Bernard Heisten.... How do you do?"

"I'm Zahra, It's my pleasure to meet you."

"No, the pleasure is mine since I am the one without the cut on the head." He said chuckling.

"I've read quite a bit about you... For some reason I thought you were.. taller.."

"Funny that our minds associate accolades to physical stature.. You are in physics?"

"No, I read a lot... and I lived here for a few months, several years ago when you were first building your new house.. There was quite a lot of talk about you."

"Oh Yes I know." Heisten frowned as he nodded.

"You were just ahead of the curve. Everyone seems to have changed their tune. I hope I did not drum up some bad memories for you." She offered.

"Grace is difficult to maintain when mediocrity is forcing itself upon you.. I was able to maintian mine." The old physicist noted. Before returning to lighter conversation "You're here on holiday then?"

"Yes, of course, just for the week... some climbing hopefully"

"You'll have to excuse me, but what was your name again?.. I have a head for theory but names escape me. "

"Zahra, Zahra Telesco."

"Telesco, do I know this name?"

Zahra lifted her pant leg and exposed his prosthetic limb.

"You may know it from the local papers... I had a little mishap a few years ago."

Heidi gazed at in awe tugging at her grandfather's pant leg and whispering up to him that Zahra had a "Fake leg".

"Hiking accident." Zahra said with a smile and tone meant to demonstrate her comfort with the injury.

"No this is not it... I know that name from somewhere else"

"It was my stepfathers name, he sold those get rich quick books. Do watch any late night TV?"

"No this is still not how I know this name… Telesco… I am thinking something to do with electronics."

"My grand father, Kenneth. He owned half of 'Integrated electronics'"

"Ah yes… I studied some of his work on low voltage resistance, for a project I worked on…. This was many years ago…. He is a good man… good ideas"

"WAS a good man…. liver failure two years ago." informed Zahra.

"Ah it's too bad we can not live forever."

'Yeah but at least he outlived his worthless son' Zahra thought to herself.

Zahra noticed that Heidi was still staring at her now covered prosthetic.

"That kite looks like its seen better days." Zahra noted as she glanced at Heidi clinging to her grandfather's leg.

"Can I see it?"

Heidi reluctantly handed over the kite. It was fashioned from a single stick split from each end toward the middle to create two forks. A string bowed the stick into its curved shape. On top of this shape a sheet of paper from a shopping bag was mounted and cut to form. It was a simple construction from recycled material.

"You know the card store in town has some really neat kites for sale." Zahra offered to Heisten.

"No she is young; she needs to see the simple way. I show her how easy it is to make a flying a machine and it takes the mystery out of it.."

"I guess your right"

"You need to break it down, show them how it works with just a piece of paper and some string. Show them with things they know, then they see it's not some magic or created by special machines."

"Sounds like you've done a lot of teaching?" Zahra inquired.

"I have two other grand children..... That is all the teaching I need..... Right Heidi?... What did we learn today?"

"I dunnno" Heidi responded shyly; her discomfort around strangers apparent.

"We learned about the diminution of air pressure above an object right?"

"yeah"

"And what does that cause."

".... Lift" Heidi eventually released.

"Very good! Bernard exclaimed. "Such a smart girl!"

"I'm impressed" Zahra said with a nod of approval.

"It is not hard you just have to simplify things, a force of nature anyone can harness in a paper bag, you see?" Postulated Heisten

"Ms Telesco it was nice to meet you.. We have more lessons to teach, so we must go." Bernard said as he offered Zahra his hand again.

"It was a pleasure"

"Come now, we learn more" Bernard said as he swept up Heidi in his arms and carried her off.

Zahra returned to gathering wood still amazed at the chance meeting that had just taken place.

An hour later a revived and freshly showered Zahra emerged from the chalet and the made her way into town. After her late start the town was mostly deserted. The serious sportsmen were up at dawn to get a full day of hiking or skiing. The lifts to the summit opened in the dim light of eight am, as the sun still hid behind the high mountain peaks. Even the "late sleepers" were still usually out on the mountain by ten.

Two of the four sporting goods stores in Mornel were run by the Needlin family. The one Zahra headed for was run by Peter Needlin, son of Authur Needlin. Peter was a pleasant, stocky man with a salt and pepper mustache. She had patronized Peter's store at the insistence of Andrew and several experience alpinists she had met. The reason the experience alpinists preferred his shop was immediately apparent. He was knowledgeable, courteous and had a warm presence about him that made his shop feel like a home. The elder Needlin sat in the corner of the store at a small table most of the day refolding sweaters. Peter had taken the time, on that first visit, to give Zahra the run down of the local politics and the history of the town. He was quite open even when talking about his own fathers troubles with Bernard Heisten. Upon entering the store Peter looked at Zahra with a hint of recognition. It only took him a second or two to pull Zahra's name from some recess of his brain.

"Ms Telesco, how are we this afternoon." Peter chimed while subtly glancing at Zahra's gate to survey the damage he had only read about.

Zahra felt like a "regular". It was a feeling Peter tried to instill in all his customers, and was no doubt the reason for the loyalty of his patrons.

"Very well peter."

"The Pleasure is mine" Peter chuckled as he shook Zahra's hand.

"How's business?" Zahra asked

"Been a warm summer you know."

"I've heard."

"Brought more people up to the cool air for now, but it doesn't bode well for the ski season."

"Well I hope it cools down for you"

"I hope so too. The glaciers rolled back further than it's been in thirty years."

Peter sighed.

"What has it been three years? No trouble with the utility knife you bought last time?" Peter added

Zahra smiled with amazement at Peter's ability to remember her last purchase, but her face sank as she came to realize the answer to his query;

"No.. actually I lost it."

Zahra had lost the knife somewhere between her free fall and the hospital. Peter read the look on Zahra's face and quickly made the connection. He would change the topic quickly.

"Well we got plenty of the latest gear here, no matter what you need"

"What I need today is some equipment for a glacier hike."

"You've certainly come to the right place."

The elder Needlin was struggling to get out of his chair as Peter stepped out from behind the counter and glass display case. Zahra had already spotted the items she'd needed in just casual glances around the store, but preferred to let Peter do the job he seemed to so enjoy. Zahra's eye lingered on the fresh assortment of Navigation and survival gadgets in the glass display.

"A pair of crampons first.. I guess"

Peter led Zahra to a wall the crampons hung from, as he instructed Zahra on the condition of the mountain.

"Glaciers rolled back nearly a hundred meters with all this heat. It will probably be soft enough that you won't really need these, but it won't hurt to have them either. It's the area between the moraine and the glacier that will be tricky"

85

"What's between the moraine and the glacier?" Zahra inquired.

Peter continued: "Well the rock that breaks off the mountain as the glacier slides down finds its way to the bottom of the ice and rubs the surface rock like a giant sheet of sand paper. Eventually the boulders are deposited on the rocky slope of the moraine. But in hot seasons like this, the glacier rolls back to expose smooth sheets of surface rock. You combine that with the melt waters and you end up with long stretches of dangerously slippery rock..... What are you a size eight? Ladies?"

"Yeah"

"got those in the back.. give me a minute" Peter said as he ducked behind a curtain to a storage area.

Zahra had meandered back to the glass case and begun examining a digital altimeter/thermometer/chronograph, when a raspy voice whispered in her ear;

"It's come'n down you know."

Zahra turned to see the crinkled face of Authur Needlin staring back at her. In front of his left eye the rickety fingers of his hand formed a "c" shape around a silver pocket watch.

"Excuse me?" Zahra replied.

Peter having heard Zahra's inquiry and thinking it was directed at him turned and spotted his father. He immediately left his work to attend to the old man.

"He's just a little senile these days. RIGHT FATHER." Peter exclaimed loud enough to register in the well stretched ear drums of the eighty eight year old. Authur mumbled as his hand found a pocket for the silver watch. He maintained eye contact with Zahra as his son escorted him back to his sweater folding station.

"Had to pick him up the police station yesterday... It's getting tough with him these days" Peter whispered as he returned to her side.

Zahra purchased a relief map for the hike and Peter was kind enough to detail a path up to the lowest of the six peaks surrounding the town. The path would circumambulate the town as it trailed back down to the opposite side. With a quickly formulated plan in hand, and her new crampons firmly attached to the outside of her bright orange backpack, she bid Peter adieu. She could only return an awkward wave to the old man as his eyes followed her out the door.

The hot afternoon sun was beating down on the glaciers that oozed over the western peaks. At he glaciers edge a tiny glint of silver the size of a small coin was beginning to poke through the ice and snow.

Zahra's hike would begin by following the tight cobble stone roads to the western edge of town, where a thin trail cut through the woods. The town would disappear amongst the trees, not to be seen again until the trail deposited her at the foot of the moraine. The sun was bright, but the air was cool and thin as she ascended the mountain. Most of the mammals became crepuscular during the summer months, so few animals crossed her path at midday. Zahra took pictures of everything she spotted. It was as majestic as she had remembered.

Upon clearing the woods she decided to take a rest on one of the large rocks that spotted the moraine. Some tiny pink and white alpine flowers grew at the foot of the rock that seemed defiantly out of place with their rocky surroundings. Zahra was careful not to disturb them. As she sucked water from a hose fed by her pack she looked around for other hikers. There were none. It amazed her that with the hundreds of hikers she knew were in town she could walk for hours and see no one. The mountains were just that huge. Her eye did catch a small pile of rocks neatly stacked in a pyramid at the foot of a giant boulder. She remembered that these stacked rocks signified the spot at which a hiker or skier met his end.

She thought for minute about the stack laid for Andrew. She wondered if she would find it. She thought about how she had met Andrew Vokun.

On the day of her awakening she had cleaned herself up in the Train station bathroom, and jumped on the next cog train from Brig to Mornel. She was still under the weather but had recovered most of her senses by the time she reached Mornel that first time. She spotted the large bulletin board outside the train station that was free for anyone to post a bill or message. Zahra stared at the cryptic notes searching her brain for the right word for "apartment". She turned from her task as she heard the clanking of metal carabineers banging against one another, approaching from her right. The noise came from the gear dangling from Andrews pack, as he strode down the main street toward Zahra. He was tall and confident. He smiled at Zahra as he passed, and she smiled back. Zahra was still perusing the message board twenty minutes later when Andrew tapped her on the shoulder

"A room you are looking for?" He asked, exercising his rudimentary translation skills. Zahra remembered the flag stitched to her backpack and was thankful someone was addressing her in native tongue.

"Yes, thank you. Can you help me?"

"We have room, my friend and me, if you like." He continued.

Andrew would be her roommate guide and friend over the four months that followed. Zahra had hoped for him to become her lover, and believed he desired the same....

It had only been a few years but it seemed like another life to Zahra as she looked back on her first four month visit to Mornel. Zahra stared down at the patch of lichen that capped the boulder she rested on. It was a fractal pattern of life in green and red, defying altitude and temperature. Nature seemed to find any tiny niche, any foothold to populate.

Zahra negotiated her way around the large slate of smooth rock that lead up to the glacier. The glacier was soft and covered by a layer of slushy snow. Zahra walked awkwardly on the soft terrain as her prosthetic provided less feedback on the stability of the snow. She slipped on her crampons, not so much for traction, but to elevate her boots above the wet snow. The air continued to thin as she ascended the mountain. She entered the phase of her strenuous workout where their muscles felt engorged and an adrenaline brought on a mild euphoria. The alpine workout and adrenaline high, was given a surreal touch by

90

the sun glaring down and blasting back up from the clean white snow of the glacier. The intense light seemed to anesthetize Zahra's exposed facial skin to the cold gusts that blew over her face. The "classic aviator" style glasses that Zahra sported only slightly muted the bright reflection of the sun off the glacier.

Approaching the crest of the range, the glacier thinned, and there were no more crevasses. The face she approached was too steep for snow or ice to collect very long. She soon reached the top of the crest and straddled the two faces of the mountain, following the ridge to the base of the great horn. To her left the snow packed heavier on the more gradual and flat western slope. To her right the steeper and more bowl like eastern face, lead down to Mornel.

Once within twenty meters of the horns base, the wind was blocked by the massive oblique pyramid of rock. Enjoying the view, the calmer air, and having been hiking for almost three hours, Zahra decided to break for lunch. Lunch was no more than dried fruit and nuts, and a protein bar, but the rest was welcome.

Zahra was using a new prosthetic she had been fitted with only two months earlier. It was a made from custom molded composite plastic. A silicone insert helped absorb impact on her tibia. Zahra was happy so far with the performance and comfort of the prosthetic. As she chugged some water, Zahra filed away a quick mental note on minor improvements and adjustments she would bring up with her orthopedist back home.

Eating her "meal in a bar" Zahra wondered aloud on the techniques used to produce such complete nutrition with such a long self life. Her jovial thoughts on the quality of engineered foods were quickly forgotten as her eye caught a small pyramid of stacked rocks a few meters to her left. She was in the right area of the horns base. 'It could be his' she thought. She ceased gnawing on her food bar, and collected her things.

She stood above the rock pile then gazed upward at the last vertical rock face she had ever climbed. It could have been the place he'd come to rest. The rocks could have been Andrew's memorial. She stared down at the rock pile, as a gentle wind began to tussle with her long hair.

"I'm sorry." Escaped her lips.

She paused for a moment to gaze out over the range. The view would have been the last image to shoot through Andrew's brain. She soaked it in. Standing above the clouds, she could see a weather system coming in from the north. It was creeping over a distant range into some far off valley. Witnessing this movement of clouds from above, and imagining people on the ground in that distant valley being doused with a cold rain, Zahra felt like a spirit. Like a detached observer of the world. Zahra remembered one of her last nights in the apartment with Andrew.

"He looks like a guppy!" Gustaf laughed. Zahra turned slowly to notice Andrews lips perched and bulging inside the clear plastic tube, the smoke slowing turning it opaque. The ridiculous contortions of his face were accentuated by the sound of gurgling water at the pipes base. His thumb released the carburetor and quickly the tube was clear again. He looked even more ridiculous as he turn to Zahra and offered her a hit. Every muscle in his face clenched as if they could help keep the smoke in his lungs.

"Take it easy you are going to blow an o ring." Gustaf again prodded his mate from the adjacent couch.

Zahra's brain finally allowed a laugh. Her mind had been fixed on theology for the last hour, or was it ten minutes? She couldn't tell. Now she could only think about Andrew's contorted face, and guppies. Three times she subdued her laughter and tried to raise the device to her lips. Each time Gustaf had a comment that restored her fit of laughter.

"You look like a blow fish"

"Trying putting your lips around the outside… that would be diiiirrrrrtier"

"You sure you know how to work that thing?"

Zahra finally shot Gustaf an insincere glare.

"If you don't stop I'm going to come over there and dump this on you." She threatened jokingly as she held up the tubes dirty brown water for his review. Gustaf leaned back further into the couch holding his hands up in mock fear. Andrew chuckled as he leaned his head against Zahra's shoulder. Finally she got the pipe to her lips long enough to flick on the lighter.

Gustaf stood up and moved into the apartment's tiny kitchen, his lanky build visible beneath the white cloth bath robe he wore. 'He looks like a holy man' Zahra thought as she took note of his long brown hair falling down the back of the robe in gentle curls, and flapping of his sandals against the heels of his feet. Again her mind returning to theology, and the statement Gustaf had made ten minutes, or an hour, prior. 'I can tell you there definitely is a god.'

Andrew lifted his head from Zahra's shoulder; she could feel him looking at her as she placed the pipe on the small table to the right of their couch. She turned to him and it was as if he could tell her mind had return to their discussion on god;

"You will see when we climb the horn this weekend. You'll feel something." he whispered to her.

"So whose god is the right god?" Andrew called just loud enough for Gustaf to hear across the tiny apartment.

"No ones.... Or everyone's." Gustaf responded as he returned to the living area with a bowl of brightly colored cereal.

"Everyone who's thought freely and then found there own god, they have the right god. If your vision of god is completely defined by an organized religion.." He paused taking a heaping spoonful of the cereal into his mouth, "chances are you got the wrong god." He continued mumbling though his cereal.

"How do you explain so many people believing in the Messiah, feeling like they have been touched by him?"

"Tell me these aren't the tastiest little fuckers?" Gustaf exhaled as he passed the cereal bowl to Zahra.

Zahra's taste buds tingled like never before as a blast of fruity aromas filtered through her nostrils. They were in fact 'tasty little fuckers'. The sugary puffs crunched beneath her molars.

"Everyone has these moments like when your child is born or when you've reached the top of a summit and you feel this sense that god is with you and you feel touched.... Hey get your own." Gustaf paused to retrieve his cereal bowl from Zahra who was shoveling down her fifth heaping spoonful.

"In those moments you notice it and you tie the image of god you've been indoctrinated with to that feeling." he concluded.

Zahra had long ago concluded that no god would allow the abuse she had endured, or if he had then she had no desire to pay homage to him. There were however moments, like this one, when her disbelief wavered. She gazed over at Andrew, she loved his gentle patient nature, she was happy around him. He often tried to get her to attend church. She decided now that maybe she would give it a try, it seemed to bring him a solace she wished that she could attain. She was in one of the most beautiful places in the world, she had made good friends, and damn that cereal was tasty. Her brain still processed the sweet signals lingering on her taste buds.

Andrew turned to Zahra and the two shared a smile. Andrew had resolved to 'make his move' with her as soon as his friend had finished his three week stay. Gustaf would be leaving on the morning of Zahra's first attempt at the great horn.

"It's a failure of perspective that kills us." Gustaf noted after slurping down the remnants of his cereal.

"All around the word people are feeling the same thing in those moments. Even if you think it's just a sense of ……connectedness, and there's nothing more mystical about it, or if you think it's a divine presence, it's really the same thing for every religion. It should be a unifying force, maybe THE unifying force and yet because we internalize it with the god we've been indoctrinated with..... it divides us." Gustaf thought out loud.

"You gotta stop smoking this shit, you're thinking too hard." Andrew responded.

"The only reason this shit is illegal is because it makes you concentrate on a topic for long time. You smoke and read the paper or a book; suddenly you start to see how the machine works..... nobody wants you see how the machine works. The worker bees might loose their motivation... This shit gives me, and my taste buds, a heightened sense of awareness. What else you got to eat?"

"Fuck'n free loader. When are you leaving again?" Zahra jibed as she tossed a pillow at Gustaf.

"Hey you're going to miss me when I leave and you're stuck with him to entertain you." Gustaf returned.

"We'll see." Zahra snapped.

"I wish I could stay an extra day and do the horn with you guys." Gustaf added returning to a serious tone.

"Yeah it's too bad it cost so much to change your flight." Andrew noted feigning sincerity as he thanked his god that Gustaf was finally returning home. He loved him like a brother but preferred to share his time in smaller doses.   His presence in the tiny apartment was also hindering the burgeoning romance between him and Zahra.

"Don't let this guy get you killed Zahra." Gustaf joked as he took the bong in hand again and pressed it to his lips.

"I trust him." Zahra smiled.

Zahra broke from her trace-like state to notice the western peaks were already throwing their shadow down the mountain. She would be running out of daylight soon. The wind tugged lightly at the relief map as she quickly verified her path home.   Peter had highlighted all of the trails she could take should she need a quick exit from the mountain.   Zahra spotted a trail that ran down along the edge of another glacial flow that would bring her back to the side of town opposite the chalet. She could then walk along the lighted streets most of the way to her temporary home.   This glacier had some visible crevasses that, although not wide, still had to be navigated carefully.

Zahra was beginning to feel the effects of the altitude and physical activity. Within an hour she had descended to the edge of the glacier, which ended in a head wall about a meter tall.   Her tired legs were beginning to shake.   Approaching the edge she dropped to her knees to climb off the head wall backward. Turning her back downhill she shimmied off the headwall, leading with her organic limb. It was then that a tiny glint of silver caught her eye. It was not a bright glint in the half light of the setting sun, but enough to catch her attention as she bent down. It was only a meter and a half from the edge of the glacier. Zahra reached out and touched the silver object and found that it did not budge. Now leaning over the object, Zahra started to uncover it. It appeared to be a curved pipe, sticking up out of the ice. She continued to clear away the thin layer of loose snow, but the pipe penetrated into the solid ice under-layers of the glacier.

Zahra sat at the base of the glacier and removed her crampons then returned to hack at the ice around the object, using the spiked tip of the crampon. Through the clearer ice she could see hints that the device penetrated deeply into the glacier. And there appeared to be a sphere attached to the underside of the pipe. It showed no rust, and was as clean and shinny as surgeon's steel. The steel spikes of the crampon grazed the metal protrusion accidentally and she stopped her hacking for moment to inspect the damage. Not a scratch had been made. Her crampons were high carbon steel. There were only few materials she knew of that were harder. It seems to be some super hard chrome-like alloy.

Tired and perplexed she stared at the exposed section of the metal thing. What ever the thing was, it was clearly out of place. The light continued to fade as Zahra searched her mind for an explanation. Meteorological equipment, intelligence gathering devices, Military weapons, none of it seemed plausible. There was no rust, no burn marks one would expect to find on a satellite that had re-entered the atmosphere. The luster of the metal was unlike any metal she had ever seen, it appeared chrome like in direct light but diffracted a rainbow of colors when the light struck it at an acute angle. After a moment, Zahra decided she did not have the tools to excavate the site, nor did she have the time in the fading light. She would have to come back, if she wanted to dig out more of the mysterious object.

Zahra made it down the remaining four kilometers in record time. Along the way exploring her mind for possible origins of the device, and making a shopping list of things she'd need to excavate the site. She'd need a pick axe, and maybe a torch to melt away the ice close to the surface of the device, as not to scratch it. The LED headlamp she had brought needed batteries. Zahra added these to the list in her head. She would also need to fashion a litter upon which to carry the device down. Zahra added two strong poles and some rope to her running list. She detoured two blocks from her route home to hit the hardware store.

The hardware store was ten minutes from closing as Zahra entered. She quickly found all the tools on her mental list. Zahra also grabbed a canvas sack in which to place any fragments of the object in the event it were not intact.

The hospital's diagnostic wing was quiet. Most of the lights were off except for the MRI room, where M.E. Jenna Wright was working into the night. The straightened but still grotesquely deformed body of Beth Needlin lay on the sliding plastic gurney of the MRI machine. The cadaver inched its way into a tunnel of light and electromagnetic energy. Jenna studied the images at the MRIs console. Inch by inch cross sections of the corpse flashed across the monitor. Jenna was focused on shattered bones of Beth's spinal column as she jotted notes referencing the image numbers being displayed on the screen. The roomed gently hummed with the noise of hard drive bearings and power supply fans. As the laser line drawn by the MRI approached the butterfly shaped scarring on the corpse's abdomen, the images became more and more distorted.

Jenna saw only a "system error" message as she tried to recalibrate the machine to a discernable image.

Beneath the corpses skin the electromagnetic energy of the MRI surged through an unseen conductive filament that just barely poked through the dead skin. A tiny package of complex electronics processed the energy and retransmitted a signal back out through same thin antennae embedded in the cold grey flesh.

Nearly three kilometers away, in the belly of the device that protruded from the glaciers edge, a circuit switched on.

IV: Preservation

Zahra was exhausted by the time she returned to the chalet. The room had cooled substantially since the wood stove was idle all day. She shook free from the bed of ashes the scant few embers that remained and nursed, with her breath, a kindling fire.

Zahra huffed and cooed as she slid between the cold sheets. The chill of the comforter quickly disappeared as her tired muscles sank into the soft feathers. Her eyes still stung from the cool dry air, wind, and intense light. They were glad to be closed.

Aching biofeedback was being channeled to Zahra's brain from every area of her body. Under normal circumstances these signals would induce a long and sound sleep, but her mind kept taking her back up the mountain to the mysterious machine that lay packed in ice at the glaciers edge. She turned to the small traveling alarm clock, which she had placed on the rail that prevented accidental falls from the loft. It was as close to her head as possible. Zahra could hear the faint ticking of its hands. She began to worry that she would knock it off while she tossed in her sleep. Then she worried about finding it too quickly in the morning and turning it off before she was sufficiently awake. She grabbed the clock, sat up, and looked for a good place to leave the clock. The moon light tossed a blue glare throughout the Chalet. Zahra leaned down to the side of the bed as far as she could, without getting out, and then pushed the alarm clock along the floor until it was just out of reach. Again she tried to sleep, but her mind was fixated on the object that hid in the glacier. She could not stop the flurry of activity in her mind. She worried about not waking up, about someone happening upon her discovery. Recognizing that her mind was working over time, her inner dialogue was a battle to calm her mind.

Though she remained still, behind her tightly shut eyes a torrent of mental activity churned. As tired as she was she could not force sleep. Something in her core character prevented her. An inner voice that told her the moment she stopped letting her mind go where it wanted, she would become ordinary. The pressures forcing her into routines grew stronger as she aged, but still that voice told her she'd start dying the moment she forced herself to sleep. Despite the tardiness problems it caused her, she thought herself better for it.

Zahra opened her eyes to find the glint of moonlight bouncing thought the chalet. She noted to herself that she might see the sunrise before her torrent of thoughts subsided, then she estimated how long it would take to return to the glaciers edge… 'An hour' she concluded.

She flexed some key muscles beneath the sheets. They ached, but she could push them.

In a matter or fifteen minutes she had the new pick, torch and other supplies loaded in her pack, and was out the door. Though the chalet had still felt cool as she dressed, the chill of the night air was still a shock as she exited. She back-tracked exactly as she had come down, following the 'Weis' trail back up to the glacier's edge. The LED headlamp worked well and the going was easier than expected. Approaching the glacier she could feel the adrenaline picking up her energy level.

Zahra checked her watch as she hit the glaciers edge and dropped her bag. Sixty nine minutes up. She hoped to start her decent as soon as possible. She climbed up and shoveled away the loose snow she had covered the metal protrusion with. The warm weather had left the glaciers edge quite malleable, so the initial two feet of snow was easy going, as she picked from the edge of the glacier inward.

Her strokes with the pick were broad and powerful at the beginning as she knew the device was buried deep within the ice bank. She took off fairly large chunks of ice with each swing; Stopping every few minutes to clear away the debris at her feet. After clearing away about two thirds of the ice that separated her from the device, the ice took on a new consistency. It was more transparent and did not show the visible layering that a glacier normally has. She noted the change. The cycles of freezing, melting and compacting of new snow, creates distinct layers in the glacial ice. The crystalline structure of each layer aligning at different angles makes the ice opaque. The ice she was chopping at now was clear, and had been frozen at the same time. The transparent ice began to reveal the device within it. When the nearest edge of the metal device was only a thin layer of ice away, Zahra broke out the torch and melted a small patch of the ice away. With the first patch of metal exposed, she could not help but stop and touch the device with her bare hands. It was as smooth and cold as the protrusion at the top of the glacier.

Having reached the device from the side, Zahra "game planned" for a moment, and decided to put down the torch until the entire device was freed as much as possible. She would go back to the pick, using broad strokes again to dig two channels to the left and right of the device. Eventually she'd encircle the object. Over the next hour and a half Zahra cut out a large monolith of ice in which the device was contained. Working in the "U" shaped channel that enveloped the device, she chipped away with more precision and less force. Zahra could now see the light of her lamp bouncing through the ice channel and back through the other side of the block. Her light showed the silhouette of the device rather clearly. It appeared to be a thick outer tube in the shape of an inverted tear drop. The tapered point stabbed downward into the glacier. The teardrop outline was nearly complete save a small section at the top that she had first uncovered In the middle of this form was a fairly large sphere, about the size of a beach ball. Sprinkled around the device's midsection appeared to be a fragments of rusted iron chain. Only a few links remained intact and those crumbled even with gentlest stroke of the pick. The joints of her back popped, as she stood up from the hunched position she had been working in. She stretched the kinks out, as she admired the progress she had made. A quick time check showed the she had been hacking at the glacier now for three hours. She would put the torch to work from here.

"I still have no idea what this thing is?" Zahra mumbled to herself.

She planned to leave a small section of ice at the bottom to hold it in place until she figured out how to brace it and haul it out. She wondered how old the ice she had been excavating was.

"Maybe it's a satellite fragment that came in hot hit he glacier and melted itself into the ice." Zahra speculated to herself

"But the rusted iron chain links that seem to surround it" She continued to ponder the

108

device.   The chain was rusted into dust in many spots.

"That type of complete rusting would take decades." She thought.

The torch sparked back to life. Zahra was careful not to keep the torch on any one area for more than a second or two. She could tell the exterior was metal but there might be flammable components under the metal skin.   The light of the flame from her side of the ice block bounced back through to show the device's form clearly. She had no desire to waist time admiring it, as the long hard day was beginning to take its toll.   She put her torch to work melting away what remained of the ice encrusting the strange machine.   Zahra gathered sections of the rusted metal chain as they fell from the ice block, and placed them in the canvas sack.

By four thirty in the morning she had nearly completed the job, only a few small chunks of ice clung to the hollow area between the sphere and tube sections. Zahra shut off her torch and admired the form that stood before her. Examining now the whole of the structure, she could see no obvious function for it. It stood before now in the alcove of ice like a modern art sculpture. Zahra pulled a wedge of ice out from the tight section where the sphere met the tubes that made up the point of the teardrop. She examined it in her hand and noticed what appeared to be black animal hair a few centimeters below the surface.   Gently picking at the ice wedge Zahra believed she had found the remnants of some kind of animal.   Zahra puzzled over the strange frozen form for a moment before deciding to leave it encased in ice for the moment. She placed it in the bag with the chain links she collected earlier. She would take it down to the chalet and keep it frozen in the ice box until she could figure out what to do with it.

Exhausted, the task before her now was getting the device down the mountain and into the chalet.

Zahra removed from her pack a large canvass tarp that had previously covered the wood pile of the chalet. She wrapped the device in it before gently rocking the device until it cracked free from the small base of ice it sat upon.   The device was surprisingly light, at about twenty five kilos.   She rested the canvas wrapped device on the bed of snow she had created during the excavation. She secured it further with rope and tape she had purchased at the hardware store.

"Now how to carry it" she asked herself.

She surveyed the hundred meters of moraine that stood between her and the beginning of the trail she had followed.   It occurred to her that she could fashion a crude litter from some fallen branches and drag the device back.   She did not care to waste time pondering other options.   She did a hurried sweep of the area to collect her gear and the canvass sack of chain fragments. She had

110

pushed herself too far and her physical condition mandated descent as soon as possible. She was beginning to loose sensitivity in her residual limb, from the exhaustion. Her steps were beginning to become unsure and wobbly. She hoisted the device to her chest. Though lighter that expected, it still placed a noticeable burden on her back and legs. She would have to drag it.

She would remember little detail of the trip down. At this point, she simply droned on in a stupor. Zahra stopped two or three times and only briefly. She decided to carry the device on the shortest route to the chalet, which took her through the center of town. The only light on the main street was from the Bakery window. The baker caught a glimpse of her staggering past his shop dragging the odd tarp-covered payload. She resembled a weary tribesmen returning to the village with a kill, hastily strapped to large pine branch.

Zahra's prosthetic collapsed beneath her, as she fell through the door of the chalet. The canvas wrapped mass dropped to the floor with a thud.

The pained look on the face of Marcus gave way to a giant sigh, and then a wry smile. Adeline rubbed her breasts against Marcus as she slid her way up Marcus's torso. She kissed her way up the wedge of chest exposed by his unbuttoned shirt. She moved steadily upward until reaching his neck, whereupon Marcus pushed her away. Knocking Adeline to the floor he zipped his pants, and buckled the thick utility belt that seemed to hold together the tight midsection of his police uniform.

"Clean yourself up before you kiss me." Adeline's stare pierced the back of Marcus' head. The hate in her gaze was dulled by the youthful glow of her round face.

Marcus knew her anger would soon yield to her need for acceptance. He knew her type, the infinitely exploitable. Adeline, born to poverty, had come to Mornel at the age of sixteen as Ski season help at a local tavern. She never left. For his part, Marcus had been indoctrinated very early into strict adherence to scripture. Scripture twisted over centuries to serve the political interests of the times. Written, re-written, still touted as 'the word of god'. It was easy for a man like Marcus to miss the true lessons amongst talk of concubines, rape in the country versus rape in the city, and who had begotten whom. In his mind he had a right to mistress. Scripture told him so.

Marcus opened the paper bag Adeline had left on the chair for him. He began examining the contents. Adeline entered the small private bathroom that attached to Marcus' office, as Marcus began eating his croissant.

"Will I see you after work?" Adeline called from bathroom. Marcus ignored her as he continued eating.

Adeline emerged from the bathroom her waitress uniform now tucked and buttoned around her voluptuous body.

Approaching Marcus from the side she placed one hand on his penis, and the other on his rear. "Big daddy wanna play some more?" she whispered seductively arching her head upward toward his.

Marcus quickly grabbed Adeline by her hair with his left hand, and covered her mouth with his other. He backed her quickly against the bathroom door she had just emerged from.

"Did I tell you about talking in this office?" Adeline closed her eyes and nodded a "yes"

"Only whispers right?" he pulled down hard on her hair to punctuate his point. Adeline grimaced in pain and grabbed momentarily at his hand.

"These walls are thin I can't have other people in this office knowing I spend time with sluts like you."

Marcus again punctuated his statement with a jerk of Adeline's hair. Her eyes swelled with tears.

"Now when I take my hand off your mouth I want you to whisper that you're sorry."

Adeline nodded a 'yes' and Marcus slid his hand from her mouth maintaining his grip on her hair. Adeline gasped a barely audible

"I'm sorry" before Marcus jerked her head back.

"You better be!" Marcus spewed in Adeline's ear, as his now free hand groped beneath her skirt.

"I'm sorry." Adeline quickly forced out in another whisper.

"That's right... You feel wet, you been with someone else? huh?"

"Nooo never" Adeline gasped, as tears continued to stream down her face.

"Who owns you slut?" Marcus demanded.

"You do. " Adeline exhaled just as Marcus began to tug again at her hair.

"That's good... now assume the position." Marcus said as he released his grip.

Adeline stepped cautiously over to Marcus's desk still sobbing softly. She hiked up her skirt as she bent over the desk. Marcus mounted Adeline and began pumping his pelvis into her diminutive body. Her face, unseen by Marcus, was twisted in pain.

Zahra had fallen to the sleep of someone who had pushed her body to the limits of human endurance. By the time she

116

had reached her bed the auroral sun had already begun to bounce off the cloud cover and fill the valley with ambient light. Hours later the hard sun light was cracking over the peaks and blasting thought the old painted windows of the chalet.

The bright light was no match, however, against the fatigue that pinned her to the warm bed. By not firing up the wood stove before going to sleep, she had let the air temperature in the chalet approach the freezing point. Her body heat and perspiration rose through the comforters and condensed near the outer surface, making the comforter feel moist and heavy. The weight of the perspiration-laden comforter and muscle fatigue discouraged any movement under the covers. Zahra slept motionless, and exhausted.

It was not until the noon sun had crossed its apex that she found the energy to turn over on her side and peer down into the living space. Scanning the room half asleep, her gaze stopped at the spot next to the couch where she thought she had dropped the device. The device was not there, but strangely this caused her no panic. In her groggy state, the trip back up to the glacier seemed more likely a dream than reality. She returned to lying on her back and staring at the ceiling, as she reconsidered the events of the prior evening. The details were too crisp and seemed to logical to have been a dream. She was soon sure there was something amiss. She sat up and looked down again at spot where the device should have rested. The sun had already taken the most of the chill from the Chalet, but the air was still cool enough to revive her further.

Zahra slunk to the ladder and began her descent into the living space scanning the room as she descended. Upon reaching the final rung she spotted the device. It was standing against the back wall of the chalet under the overhang that created the loft space. She could not recall moving it, yet there it sat in the corner. She scanned her recollection of the prior night's events and noted that her memories were hazier as the night wore on. This fact placated her uneasy feeling for the moment, and Zahra turned her attention to the morning rituals of alpine living, albeit afternoon.

She started by clicking on the electric stove to begin warming the kettle. The air temperature in the chalet was well below comfort level, and so the iron stove needed fire. Since there was no trace of embers in the neglected stove, starting the fire took several minutes. She was still very tired, and thankful there were still a few logs and kindling left in the small rack next to the stove. She filled the iron kettle with water and, on the chalets small dinning table, laid out some rolls and preserves. Parking herself in the chair closest to the wood stove, she hunched toward it to maximize her heat absorption. Alternately her eyes gazed at

118

the device in the corner, the flickering flames through the iron stove grate, and the kettle on the stove. She encouraged the water to boil quicker with her mind, as she pulled the sleeves of her shirt over her hands, and tucked her arms tight to her body.

Soon Zahra was pouring herself a cup of tea. She sat staring at the device for a few minutes as she sipped it. It occurred to her that she was probably quite rank from the sweat and stress of the previous day and a half. As one does, she had become accustomed to her own stink, as it slowly ramped to acrid. Now that she had been reminded of bathing she sampled the air around herself with a more objective nose. It did not mix well with the preserves.

The more she thought about the device as she studied it from the kitchen table, the more she was starting to believe it was of military origin. The government was always a few years ahead on the technology curve. She tried to infer some potential military function a device of its shape would be well suited for. She thought perhaps the sphere in the center was some explosive payload. This thought sent a brief tinge of fear down her spine. The duct's that protruded from either side of the device might have severed to propel it. She again found herself temped to get up and inspect the device closer, but her stomach and the warm mug in her hands over ruled that desire. Instead she shifted the focus of her

119

thoughts to an assessment of whether or not she had done the right thing. In bringing the device down from the glacier, she had violated several ordinances by cutting away the glacier. Zahra was certain that the snow and ice she tampered with would have been melted over the remaining weeks of summer; but none the less she had accelerated the melting of that small section near the glaciers rim. Had the environment impact been truly substantial she might not have undertaken the hasty and covert excavation.

Still she could not place why she had been so anxious to secure the device. She was a visitor to this country and had disregarded a government's sovereignty in the name of discovery. She was not unaware of the risks she was taking. The device appeared to be of modern construction so she reasoned; whether the device was for military, intelligence, or of some alien origin, she could think of no scenario where she would want to turn the device over to local magistrates without first having a good look at it and documenting its existence. She decided to take out her sketch book and draw the device, as she sipped her tea.

Adeline scurried from the front door of the precinct. She had been instructed to hold the receipt and a wad of cash in plain sight. There could be no hint of impropriety as she strolled away. Marcus allowed a few minutes to pass before he stepped onto the ancient cobblestone streets. The midday sun beamed off his well polished Sheriff's star and thick golden buckle. He removed a clipboard from under his arm as he began to stroll eastward. On the clipboard was a fuzzy image in blue and red streaks. It showed the heat signature of a one legged person and a strangely shaped device.

When Zahra had gotten within a meter of the glacier she was detected. Since she was still far from the border, which ran across the top of the range, the monitoring system did not trigger an alert. When she lingered on the mountain for more than two hours the system triggered an "informational alert" to the guardsmen on duty. The guardsmen reviewing the images noted in a journal that she had not attempted to summit the mountain or cross the border.

The images of Zahra were boxy, even with the computers best enhancement. The heat escaping through seems in her clothes and her exposed face showed up as pixilated strings and spots of red and pink.

The guardsmen's initial thought was that she was a geologist or maintenance worker from the ski lift company. As she hoisted the device out of the ice and heated the device with the torch, the boxy representation of the device's outline showed up in the picture. The Guardsmen watched Zahra take her first few steps back toward town before she fell off his screen.

Had she tried to exit the country by continuing up over the range it would have been his duty to call up to the men at the summit post. Since there was no cause to believe an offense or customs violation had been committed, he took no action. He did think it strange however that a someone would be on the mountain at that hour. Since he could not identify what had been hauled down; he thought it best to give the information over to the local sheriff. He printed out the clearest frames and had them sent over to Marcus Brein.

Marcus was intrigued by the printout, but not enough to detract from his usual morning rituals. He mounted an ATV emblazed with the sheriff's department crest, and head up to the site of the "incident".

The ATV bounced along the moraine approaching the two meter square hole Zahra had made at the glaciers edge. At the very least several town ordinances, against destruction of the glacier, had been violated. Marcus dismounted and began examining the smooth ice that had been directly against the device. From the impressions left in the ice, and the infrared photo Marcus formulated picture of the device in his head. He now realized that whatever had been carried down the night before had been locked in the glacial ice. Marcus lingered at the site for a few minutes looking for anything the "suspect" might have dropped. His search yielded only a handful of boot prints, and what appeared to be a rusted pad lock that he estimated was several decades old. It also registered in his brain that the unidentified body in the morge had been recovered just a few hundred yards away.

Marcus radioed a deputy to join him at the site with a camera. The offense he was investigating did not warrant an "all out" forensic analysis. Marcus had received no reports of theft, so whatever the "suspect" had taken down from the mountain, there was no cause to turn the site into a crime scene. Marcus did harbor a contempt for visitors who disrespected "his" mountain. It also registered in Marcus's mind that someone had spent an entire night on the mountain retrieving something. The opportunist in him needed to know 'what could be worth all that trouble?' As he surveyed the excavation site he resolved to shake a few low branches.

Zahra realized the tiny hot water heater that serviced the chalet ran out quickly, as the current of cold water coming from the shower head stung her skin. Albeit short, the shower was a welcomed respite from the action of the prior two days. The cold shock that punctuated the shower served to revive Zahra, further shaking off the remnants the morning's lethargy.   She was still wrapped in a towel, and sitting on the toilet reattaching her prosthetic, when a thump at the door startled her.   The mysterious device still sat in the corner as exposed as she was.

She thought for a moment about pretending to be out.

"Zahra?" the familiar voice of Father Jolien projected through the thick wooden door.

"Shit" she mouthed in muted exclamation, as she scanned the room for something to cover the device with.

"Zahra?" again the priest called as she stumbled across the room to grab a quilt that draped the back rest cushions of the small sofa.

"Ah... I'm just getting out of the shower!... One second!" Zahra called out as she covered the device and leaned her large backpack against the now 'quilt-hooded' form.

"There's a canvass sack outside the door here." Father Jolien called out.

In their delirium the prior night Zahra had dropped the bag, with the chain remnants and the frozen furry mass, on the steps of the chalet.

"Ah.. yeah... I found that on the trail yesterday." Zahra stammered as she quickly grabbed the dirty clothes she had left in the bathroom and dressed herself.

124

The priest was peering into the canvass sack as Zahra open the door.

"Hello.. sorry about that, you caught me a bad time." Zahra apologized as the priest entered carrying the canvass sack.

"May I sit?" The priest asked.

"Sure" she acquiesced.

The grinding of the rusted iron bits could be heard as the priest dropped the canvass sack on the table. It was sopping wet. Zahra quickly deduced that the block of ice that held the furry mass had melted under the afternoon sun that hit the front of the chalet.

"Wonder what you found here." The priest queried as he delicately lifted the sack open.

"Ah…" Zahra stammered as she watched the priest's hand slowly enter the sack.

"ew!" he exclaimed "it's kind of slimy Wait a second" Jolien appeared perplexed as he groped in the sacked for long moment.

The old priest's face turned to terror as his hand began convulsing under the canvas. His entire body began to shake violently. Zahra was about to lunge at the canvas sack to restrain whatever was inside, when suddenly the priests motion stopped and he began to chuckle:

"Ha ha, I had you fooled there I did?"

"I almost had a heart attack. Come on!" Zahra exclaimed as her pulse returned to normal.

Jolien slowly removed the damp furry mass from the sack. Peeling it open exposed the leather back of what appeared to

125

be a fur coat collar.   There were some smears of wet rust on sections of the hairy swatch.

"Looks like a piece of a coat." Jolien declared.

Zahra stepped closer as the two examined the swatch in detail.

"Yeah, and it looks pretty old. See the loosely wound thread holding it together." Zahra pointed out.

"Yes, and you see.. tar residue along the seams... old fashion sealant.   Edges are hand sewn...   This is like they used to make when I was a boy." The priest added

Turning the swatch over he further noted:

"No brand or label.... Looks like this thing was handmade.... "

"The edges of the fur are crudely cut as well." Zahra noted.

"What else is in here?"   Jolien asked rhetorically as he handed the swatch of fur to Zahra, and again reached into the bag.

Father Jolien retrieved a hand full of rapidly deteriorating iron chain. Reddish brown silt covered his hand.

"You say someone just left this on the trail?" The priest asked.

"Yeah."

Zahra's lie was punctuated by the thump of her backpack falling to the ground next to the device. It had taken the quilt to the floor with it. Once again the device was exposed.

Marcus Brein swaggered through the door of the Needlin's sporting good store. Peter was closing up the shop and the elder Needlin was waiting in a chair near the door. Marcus gave Authur a respectful tip of his police cap, as he entered. The old man showed no hint of recognition, as he continued to stare off as if he could see beyond the walls of the stores.

"Good evening Peter"

"What can I do for you Marcus? This about Dad again?"

"No No, we had little incident on the mountain this morning…. Around three."

"No one was hurt I hope?"

"No, nobody hurt.. Big piece of the glacier near Cain's chute got dug up though."

"What's that got to do with me?"

"Oh nothing, nothing at all Pete…. I was just wondering if you knew anyone who'd have been headed up there early this morning."

"No.. no one I recall."

"Any idea who might have cause to go digging up a section of glacier?"

"No Marcus, all my regular customers are decent, law abiding folks….. staunch naturalists. Don't know a one who'd be up there to do damage….. I think most likely it was some kids."

"Yeah I hear what you're saying Pete, just thought I'd ask…. That's all I had."

Marcus was about to leave when he thought of another way Peter might be of some help.

"Oh Peter.. I got a picture here; maybe you can identify the object in it... Does this look like any mountaineering equipment you've ever seen?"

With that Marcus took out the infra red image showing the silhouette of the device.

"What is this?"

"It's an infrared image from the mountain last night" He added while pointing to the strange form. "Whoever was up there, they brought that down with them."

Peter looked at the image for along minute.

"No, I have no idea what that is."

"You said this was at around three or four in the morning?" Peter inquired.

"Yeah."

"Well Carl Farnaut opens the Bakery at three am.. If they came through town with this he might have seen them."

"That's a fine idea Pete.. I'll have to stop in the morning and ask him. Let me know if you hear anything. Thanks again for all your help."

Peter followed Marcus to the door gathering his Father along the way, and locked up the store.

Father Jolien stared at his morphed reflection in the curves of the device. He could see Zahra's face over his shoulder.

"No idea what it is huh?" he queried once more. Zahra was still uncertain she had done the right thing bringing the old Priest into her adventure.

"No"

"So we have that piece of fur frozen in the glacier with this thing..." Jolien thought out loud.

"Which is wrapped in an iron chain that has rusted through?" Jolien finished his thought They pulled the device away from the back wall of the chalet enough to be able to walk around it. The two circled the device as they spoke. It resembled large metallic sea horse gripping a large metallic beach ball with its proboscis and tail. The sharp crown of the device reached the priest's nose.

"And we would guess, with the rust and the construction on that swatch, at least fifty years old? Maybe seventy?" Zahra commented

"I think you are probably on the target" the Priest affirmed.

"So this thing was up there at about the same time the train here was still running on steam." Zahra said in a tone that suggested disbelief.

"That's what the evidence suggests, or we have an antique collector who wanted to get rid of some items along with this." Jolien joked.

"It looks as though this thing is a whole… I mean to say it doesn't look like a part to something else." Zahra observed.

"I agree, I don't see where it would attach to something."

"What do you think this is?" Zahra chimed as she pointed to the long probe like extension that ran along the base.

"It kind of looks like two skinny fingers, pinching a ball; when you look at it from the side." noted Zahra as she grabbed her sketch pad and began writing notes.

"It's the strangest thing I've ever seen. The luster coming off this thing seems to change with the slightest movement." she continued.

"All the vents on this thing appear to be closed, these ducts at the base the 'rear ducts' rear ducts I guess we could call them?"

"Posterior is more scientific name, but how can we be sure that's the rear of this thing." Zahra questioned.

"Well that dark plate in the front, it makes that side different from the rest." He continued.

They both stood in the newly defined "front" of the device looking closely at the curved 'plate'. A stretched image of Zahra and Father Jolien reflected off the dark glossy surface of it as Zahra continued:

"I mean if this thing is supposed to move, maybe that's its 'eye'…"

From the layout of the ducts and the position of what they believed was the devices 'eye' they again pondered the purpose of the device. They tried peering inside the ducts but found them closed by a plate of the same chrome-like material of the outer shell. They tried to gently push the plates open with their fingers, but they did not budge. Every apparent opening in the device seemed to be locked down.

Father Jolien turned the back of the device out toward the living space to get better light on it.

"What's that" Zahra's younger eyes had spotted the series of small pinholes he had missed. There were five of them in a 'X' pattern. Four holes in each corner of an invisible square, with the fifth hole in the center. This tiny configuration of openings was in the back of the device near the top of the section newly dubbed the 'pointer base'. Jolien took a closer look at the holes and still couldn't tell if they were openings or just black spots on the outer coating. He rubbed the spots with his hand to see if they would come off. They did not rub off, and she again noticed something his eyes had missed; when Jolien rubbed the surface, faint symbols appeared in a white glow around the holes. It seemed as though the heat from Jolien's hand trigger a luminescent paint under the surface enamel that would glow for a few seconds before fading back into invisibility. Zahra suggested turning out the lights and rubbing again to see if it would be more plainly visible in the dark. In the darkness glowing white symbols were plain even to the aging eyes of Father Jolien. Not wanting to drown out the image with ambient light; Zahra retrieved the headlamp flashlight. She quickly made an enlarged sketch of the symbols. The Symbols were so simple that it did not take her long to recreate them. Jolien rubbed his hands allover the device trying to elicit additional symbols from the surface, but nothing else appeared.

With the lights back on, the two stared at the cryptic sketch. Zahra soon recognized two of the symbols were diagrams of elements. She was not sure which elements, as it had been a long while since her last chemistry class. The top two holes in the five hole layout were joined by a single straight line. The bottom two holes were also joined by a single line. The center hole, or fifth hole, had no adjoining lines. The atom with seven protons was drawn in the center of the two adjoined holes at the top. The atom with six protons was drawn beneath the bottom two holes. There were two lines emanating from each atomic diagram that seemed to point toward the holes they were closest to. At the end of these lines a varying number of hash marks were drawn.

Before Zahra and Jolien had noticed, it was late in the evening. They had been toying with the device for nearly five hours, and still had no answers to the puzzling diagram.

"Have you eaten?" Jolien reminded Zahra that the restaurants would soon stop serving. Having slept into the late afternoon Zahra had only been awake for six hours or so. Zahra agreed that they should get out of the chalet and get some food. The two found their way to the nearest tavern and requested an out of the way booth.

Marcus Brein returned home, his mind still scanning his memory for where he'd seen the strange symbol in the infrared picture before. His wife Madeline greeted him at the door to take his jacket and hand him the day's mail. It was part of the rigid schedule that was her life with Marcus. Madeline was in her late twenties and glowing in the way that only pregnant women do. Her glow tainted though by a underlying sadness. Juxtaposed to her thin and petite frame was the roundness of her belly seven months pregnant. Marcus acknowledged her with a cold kiss "hello", while grabbing the infrared image from the pocket of his jacket before she pulled it away.

Marcus surveyed the house as he made his way to the large leather chair he called his own. He called it all his own. Madeline scurried over to kneel at his feet, and begin removing his shoes.

"The box of candy that was on that table is gone?" Marcus asked as he glared down at Madeline.

"Yes" Madeline replied sheepishly

"Did you eat them?"

"There were only two pieces left." Madeline added in the same sheepish tone.

"One or a dozen you are already too fat to be eating candy."

Madeline knew better than to argue.

"I am going to forgive you tonight but you'll have an additional ten pages of scripture for tomorrow. I trust you read your scripture today?"

"Of course dear.." Madeline responded as she placed his shoes next to the large stone fireplace that centered the room. The remnants of a larger fire glowed beneath the iron rack. Marcus lectured Madeline as she rekindled, restock, and bellowed the fire back to a respectable blaze.

"In your scripture today; what did you read about offering a blind or infirm animal as a sacrifice to God?" Marcus queried.

"God does not like it?" Madeline answered still attending to the fire.

"That's right. It does not show respect as a servant of God to give him anything second rate... Now scripture also tells us that as my wife you serve me... So how is it that when I come home, the fire is not already tended to? Do you think you are giving me all the respect I deserve?" Marcus sneered.

"I am sorry dear.. Tomorrow I'll be better…. Would you care for a gluvine dear?" She offered turning to Marcus with a worried expression. Marcus returned an angry stare as he considered a punishment for Madeline. After a tense moment he simply nodded a "yes", before dismissing Madeline to the kitchen.

Marcus stared at the fire as he thought again about the picture. It had conveyed an illogical sense of foreboding inside him the moment he had seen it. There was something about it, and he did not have the information he needed to put the pieces together yet. He would have to wait until tomorrow, until he could determine who it was on the mountain. His head angled back against the leather chair, upward toward the mantle, and Marcus slowly closed his eyes. His brain stirred as he contemplated sleep.

Marcus opened his eyes somehow sensing Madeline standing next to him. Maybe it had been the slight jingle of the petite silver spoon against the delicate tea cup. Perhaps it was the sweet smell of the hot spiced wine that aroused his senses. Marcus received the toddy with a dismissive nod and Madeline quickly took her leave. The wine slid down his throat warm and sweet and erased what memory there was of long day of cold dry air. He sipped with his eyes closed, his minds eye still focused on the device.

135

After a moment he opened his eyes to place the cup down on the small table beside his chair.   There on the table was a black and white photo of Marcus's father and grandfather, held up by a freestanding frame. His father looked out from the frame as a young boy of twelve, taking a knee to prop up the antlers of a slain six point buck. Grandfather appeared in his thirties and kneeled in kind directly behind his son. Marcus had seen the picture a thousand times before, but now with thoughts of the device in Marcus's head, something else in the photo stood out.   Cradled in his Grandfathers arms was the old flint lock hunting rifle that had been passed through generations of Breins, and resided at this moment in the gun closet of Marcus Brein.

He stood up hastily and crossed the room to his gun closet. He opened the door and pulled out a long scroll of felt that wrapped his heirloom rifle.   Placing the scroll on the floor near the fire, he gently unwrapped it.

He knew now why the image had seemed so familiar to him.

"The gun". He muttered staring at the old flintlock rifle. The ancient double barrel rifle nearly spanned the width of the mantle. Polished and preserved, it had been his Grandfathers passed down from his father. It had been years since Marcus had taken it out to handle it.   He took a wide handle on the stock and barrel of the antique weapon, as he lifted it off the bed of green felt.   He was always amazed by the weight of it, and how substantial it felt in his hands.

He examined the butt end of the rifle in the flickering fire light.   Years of polishing and handling had obscured the carving on the widest part.   Marcus examined the surface closely. Under the polish and stains he could see clearly fifty six hash marks, and a symbol that resembled and incomplete eye.

His father had explained that the slash marks on the butt were cut in by his grand father, each time he brought home a kill.   Marcus had noticed the eye shaped symbol before but assumed it was just an incomplete doodle from his grandfather's knife.   Marcus began to wonder if his Grandfather was connected to whatever had been pulled from the glacier.   The grandfather he never knew. His father had only stated that he had died "in the line of duty". Marcus in retrospect had come to the conclusion his father was crazy. He knew nothing of the trauma his father Edward had suffered as child.   Witnessing the violent death of his father on the glacier had been too   much.   Edward's   emotional   scars manifested themselves in a zeal for scripture, and an almost paralyzing fear that the device would one day return for him. Edward would pass this level of fear and fervor to his son. Marcus recalled feeling his father's belt when he missed church.

"There are demons in this world Marcus. You need to be ready. You need to be strong. You need to be better than the rest." He recalled his father commanding before the belt lashed his back.

He placed the rifle on the floor and in the fire-light compared the symbol to the infrared image to the butt of the gun. The shapes were a close match. Marcus was so lost in the thoughts of his grandfather that he barely noticed the phone ringing, nor did it register with him that it was quite a late hour to be receiving calls. Madeline entered with a phone and handed it to Marcus.

"Hello?"

"Marcus, it's Faulk from tower west, we got some more strange heat signals from that same spot on the mountain. Looks like there could be somebody up there again.."

Marcus was suddenly wide awake.

"Thanks, I'll check it out right now."

Before Sergeant Faulk could say another word Marcus had hung up the phone and was out the door.

Zahra and Father Jolien had just returned from dinner. Unbeknownst to them, the doors inside the ducts of the device slowly and silently spun open like the iris of a camera. The sphere at the center of the device began to spin like a top, slowly gaining speed.

They were busy puzzling over the confusing diagram as they sat at the chalet's only table.

"Maybe we have to make a chemical with these elements?" Jolien inquired.

"I think one is carbon, but I don't know... It's been a while since my last chemistry class. They'd have to have the right number of electrons in their outer shell." Zahra informed the priest.

"I don't know what this means. Remember I am a priest we don't do a lot of science." The Priest chuckled.

"It's called valence... Number of electrons in the outer shell. It is a big factor in how elements combine" Zahra explained.

"OK"

"I think given the right number of each you can make a compound out of any two elements..... Where's a periodic table when you need one?" Zahra joked.

"Suppose we'd find one at the Library but even still, knowing the 'valance'" Jolien waited for Zahra's nod to confirm he had gotten the word right. " or not, do you know how to put a chemical together?"

"I've taken some chemistry classes but I can't say I'm an expert, buuu..." Zahra cut her sentence short.

Jolien looked up from the puzzle to find a shocked expression on Zahra's face as she stared wild-eyed over Jolien's Shoulder. Jolien spun around quickly to find the Device floating a few inches from him. Zahra seemed to forget how to manage her prosthetic leg in her panic. She knocked the table backward spilling two of the chairs as she stumbled away from the device, and brushed her hand against the hot iron stove. The skin of her hand sizzled against the hot iron. Jolien now found himself backed against the sink with Zahra several feet to his left. Her back pressed against the front door.

Marcus Brein's ATV bounced along the bumpy trail to the glaciers edge. Turning past a large boulder the halogen lamp on the front of his ATV lit up the crime scene and exposed the source of the heat signature the monitoring station had spotted. Three adult wolves dashed out of the hole that Zahra had created a night earlier. In a flash, they sprinted across the terminal moraine and disappeared into the pine forest. Marcus's initial disappointment immediately gave way to curiosity, as he cut his engine. He had never seen wolves congregate on the glacier at that hour. Their prey was in the forest, and they generally stayed away from the glacier in the coldest part of the evening.

He approached the hole with his flash light drawn. There was a small patch of dark material in the center of the hole. Marcus gingerly stepped into the pile of snow that had been spilled from the glacier's edge. His "beat" shoes did not provide great traction in the muddied and melting snow. Squatting down at the entrance of the snowy alcove Marcus had his flash light focused on a cylindrical object with a dark and wrinkled exterior.   Marcus picked it up with his gloved hand and spun the tube shaped object in his fingers.   On the back there was a fingernail attached.   Marcus suddenly realized he was holding a petrified human finger.   He dropped it quickly, wiping his hand against his pant leg.   Panning the ground, he searched for more remains, then turned his attention to glacier walls.   As the beam of light hit the glacier just a few inches from his left shoulder, a human skull seemed to scream out at Marcus from under an inch of ice.   He recoiled at the sight.   What skin remained on the skull was discolored to the same cold gray as the finger.   The shattered jaw of the desiccated skull was cocked in a gaping scream.

The device slowly and silently rose over the table.   Some sort of energy poured from the ducts behind and beneath the device, as the air around it wavered like summer air over sun baked asphalt.   Zahra and the priest were held speechless by the impossible silence and fluidity of the machine's motion.   Slowly, it turned toward Father Jolien and descended off the table in

his direction. He tightened with fear...
From the proboscis that extended from
beneath the machine a sudden burst of
purple light blasted at Jolien. The startled
priest looked down at his shirt to find a grid
drawn across his body in violet laser light.
Another blast of red light emanated from the
machine and Jolien watched as a horizontal
laser line moved down his body. As soon as
the red laser line hit the floor, both lights
turned off. The device levitated within
inches of Jolien for a moment, as if deciding
what to do next. Zahra and the priest shared
a glance that communicated mutual shock
and incertitude, before returning their focus
to the device. It now turned toward Zahra,
and slowly moved in her direction. Zahra
was now packed tightly against the front
door. She reflexively held her burnt hand
over her heart, as if praying. The machine
inched to within arms length of Zahra and
stopped. She exhaled for moment before
being blasted with the same violet and red
laser light Jolien had been exposed to. This
time, however, the scanning red line stopped
at Zahra's knees and proceeded back up her
body until it reached her ribs. In an instant
the light was gone, and again the machine
was motionless.

Jolien was now behind the device,
still frozen by the shock of what he was
witnessing. The Device lunged forward at
Zahra. Its "eye" grazed Zahra's cheek as she
turn her head away from the device, and

pressed her body into the door. The proboscis pressed against the exposed skin between her tee shirt and the top band of her loose fitting sweat pants. The opening in the proboscis again emitted a violet light that seemed to penetrate Zahra's skin. She felt a warm sensation then a pinch, as the machine suddenly backed away. Reflexively she moved her hand to her abdomen; to the spot she had felt the pinch. The machine moved slowly backward, rising over the table again, and settling back in the corner it had originally rested. Zahra looked down at her abdomen and found a small welt from which a tiny glob of blood oozed. The old priest was still watching the device but edging toward Zahra, and the front door. He grabbed her by the arm, and guided her away from the door enough to open it. The two slowly backed out of the chalet, all the while keeping both eyes locked on the device... The machine began to rise again just as the two cleared the front door. The machine's movement was enough to send them scurrying out onto the mountainside. They ran several meters before ducking behind a boulder.

They peered out from behind the boulder, watching from afar as the device slowly floated through the open front door. It paused in the threshold for moment before it coasted away in the opposite direction, and disappeared into the night.

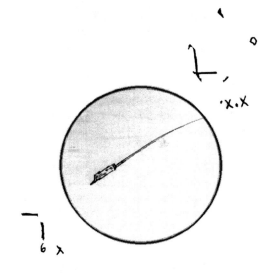

VI : Celestial Mechanics

Zahra hugged the thick comforter as she stared at the abstract forms painted on Father Jolien's bedroom wall by the stained glass window behind her.   She knew the image was of the messiah. On a rock His arms spread delivering his message.   The polygons of white brown, red and gold fell awkwardly across the contours of the varnished wooden door and the molding that surrounded it.   The form reminded Zahra of Gustaf in his bathrobe as she and Andrew joined him in discussing god.

Zahra had finally retrieved her own bowl of 'tasty little fuckers', and sat next to Andrew as she finished them.

"Do you believe in God Zahra?" Andrew asked.

"No, I can't say that I do." Zahra responded between bites.

"No heaven?" Andrew added.

"Nope."

"So what keeps you from stealing or killing? If this life is all you've got why not just take whatever you want?" Andrew continued.

"Maybe she feels she'll live on through her children, and she wants a better world for them."   Gustaf chimed in from across the table.

"I don't know that I want any..."she said before finishing with a soft "maybe."

"No?" Andrew noted, shooting Zahra a quizzical glare.

"I probably will have a kid at some point... I just don't think about being a mother much. But if you want to know why how I can lead a moral life with a religion... all I can say is; I'm just built this way. Hurting people doesn't feel good to me, and if it did I don't think an old book would get me to stop." She opined

"I know you have good heart Zahra; I do wish you would believe. It's not really about an old book... maybe on the horn you'll feel something... maybe you'll feel his presence." Andrew pleaded.

"HIS presence? I'm not sure that god needs a gender, or if it would choose to be a man. ....Don't listen to this guy Zahra. We need to process spirituality in a new way that keeps is separate from our politics and our laws. That type of shit has us killing each other. That's got to be the next revolution." Gustaf ranted.

"Hey listen, I've had my moments of doubt, but either the man was the greatest magician that ever lived or he was Messiah. " Andrew retorted.

"You don't think any of the mystic stuff could be fish tales that have grown over time? You're talking about a book that's been rewritten a dozen times." Zahra asked.

Andrew was becoming defensive as Zahra and Gustaf appeared to be 'ganging up' and him and his religion.

"I know that civilization has thrived under the laws and guidelines that that 'old book' has laid down. So why change it?" Andrew snapped.

"The man you profess to believe is a god came and said 'forget the old law, I make the new law.' He said to throw out the first half of the book himself. What happens is you have the great sages come up with important messages and people believe and follow. But then the politicians get a hold on it and the message gets prostituted and twisted. Eventually you can't even recognize the original message. Then someone revolutionary comes along and says 'hold up forget all that BS just love one another, share with one another, and live in peace.' Then the cycle starts again where the powerful slowly twist it back." Gustaf continued to rant.

"I guess I'm just traditional. Don't you see any value in tradition?" Andrew asked.

"Not when it's wrong, and especially not when it's wrong and there are alternatives. There are plenty of new sages out there that we can open our ears to, and reason about spirituality. New sages with new and better tools to view ourselves and the universe around us.. like this tool." Gustaf concluded lifting the bong up for their inspection as he broke into a silly grin.

Deputy Wiess stood at the glaciers edge, watching, as Father Jolien made his way up the trail.

"I'd have sent an atv for ya!" Deputy Wiess yelled down.

"Nahh.. How do you think I've lived this long?" Father Jolien said between heavy breaths that condensed in the cool morning air. Wiess smiled as he continued to wait for the old priest.

The morning sun had not yet cracked over the peaks, so the moraine was blanketed in a grayish half-light. Jolien finally stepped onto the slushy mat of melting snow that lay before the crime scene. There was an officer snapping photos, and another gently peeling away chunks of snow and ice from around the corpse of Frank Brein. Frank's body was missing an arm as it lay face down in the bank of ice. The legs still packed in snow and the remaining arm tucked beneath the torso.

"Unfortunate chap eh?" was Father Jolien's first reaction.

"Yeah..... Glaciers just now spitting him out. God knows how long he's been frozen." Wiess added.

"Yes, he does.. " Jolien said as he unbuttoned his jacket to reveal his vestments. "Yes, he does.." Father Jolien took silent notes on the excavation site he had heard about from Zahra.

He took another step toward the corpse, and raised his hand above the skull. Wiess stepped back, as Father Jolien issued the funeral rites. After a moment Jolien's faint mumbling ceased and he turned back toward deputy Wiess.

"Thanks for coming out father....."

"Nonsense." Jolien snapped. "You'll have to get me a date that he died; perhaps I can have Father Haig look through our records for a name."

"Yeah, we'll know more when the forensics team from Brig gets here.. I was told the estimate right now is that the bodies been about seventy years old... or seventy years dead that is." Deputy Wiess replied as he offering his arm to the priest for support.

Jolien ignored the offer and slowly navigated his way off the glaciers edge and down to the trail. The deputy followed the priest for a short while.

"Father, just by chance; have you seen or heard anyone acting strange lately?"

"Son... I hear confession. I get something strange every day."

"I bet you do... but outside of that?"

Jolien stopped and turned to Wiess.

"Not that I can think of." The priest said after a pause that feigned thought.

Wiess stopped as Jolien continued down the trail.

"Are you sure you don't want a ride!" Wiess hollered after him.

Jolien continued walking away as he waved a dismissive 'no'.

The officers had finally completed excavating the body, and were about to turn Frank's body over as Wiess returned to the glaciers edge.

The two officers flipped Frank's body with a coordinated heave.

His badge had long ago detached from the front of the jacket but from the construction of the jacket and the rest of the corpse's attire the officers knew they were looking at one of their own.

Father Jolien slowly shut the thick wooden door of his private room at the rectory trying not to wake Zahra. He was unaware that she had not yet fallen asleep in the first place. It was the result of sleeping late the prior day, and the trauma she had endured. She laid awake feeling the small welt on her abdomen with her finger, and wondering why the device had poked her. What consequence might it have? Her hand was blistered and welting from the burn of the cast iron stove. Jolien had not slept either. He had been pondering all night if he had done the right thing, and he feared for Zahra's health.

"What are we going to do now?" Zahra asked as she heard the priest enter the room.

Father Jolien pulled a small stool over the side of his bed. The priest's chamber was dimly lit by the single stained glass portal, that now threw the same abstract forms across his face.

"I don't know." Jolien replied. "Do you think we should go to the hospital tell them the big story?"

"Would they believe it, or would they put us in the loony bin?"

"I think we must tell someone. Maybe you should go home today.. "

"I think I might like that.. This thing goes past normal medicine.... What ever that thing was, no medical book is going to cover it." Zahra moaned.

"This is right.. Just a general doctor is no help..." Jolien concurred.

"And the symbol… I think it's a big clue to what we are dealing with. We need a biologist.. . or a chemist or something " She added.

"Even if you could get out of here today I don't want you to wait twelve hours to have this looked at." Jolien insisted.

Zahra hated herself for not leaving the device where she'd found it. Father Jolien searched his mind frantically for a way to help the distressed girl.

"What about Dr. Heisten? He is great scientist."

Zahra's look of deep consternation shifted that the mention of the famous scientist.

"Do you think he'd help?" Asked Zahra

"There's only one way to find out" he proclaimed.

The bookshelves that lined the walls of Bernard Heisten's study were filled with bindings of leather and canvas. The embossed gold and silver lettering on the bindings twinkled in the otherwise muted atmosphere of the room. Dr. Heisten was conversing on the telephone, when he heard the intercom buzz. His daughter Laura managed the affairs of the house, so he expected she would soon attend to the visitors. He continued his conversation, until Laura entered the room.

"Father, the Priest 'Jolien' is at the gate with a girl who says she knows you… something about a kite?"

The kite reference did not register immediately.

"Oh.. Our neighbor for the week.. yes, let them in." Heisten answered after an awkward pause.

Heisten finished his conversation and placed the handset down on the small beverage table next to his oversized leather chair. He then turned his attention to the large picture window to his right. From it he could see the front gate, and he watched as the priest and Zahra hurried across the entrance of his villa. He detected an urgency in their step that made him wonder if there was something amiss.

In a moment the two were entering his study, almost pushing Laura aside in the process.

"Ms. Telesco, I believe you've broken the speed record from the gate to this room... Is something urgent?" Heisten jibed, in an awkward attempt to leaven the tense atmosphere that had just entered the room. Zahra got right to the point.

"Dr Heisten we need your help...." began the disclosure of all that they had seen and done with the device.

In the hand of Marcus Brein a Hardware store receipt detailed the purchase of a pick axe, and a torch kit. The name printed on the receipt "Zahra Telesco". He had a name... it would not be long now. Again he heard his father's voice. "There are demons in this world."

Dr. Bernard Heisten carefully guided the tweezers across Zahra's skin aided by a large swing-arm magnifying lens. From the center of the welt a thin white hair protruded. It nearly blended with Zahra's sparse and wispy body hair, except that it seemed slightly thicker and rigid. Heisten grabbed the white hair with the tweezers and pulled at it gently. He was surprised to see the hair extended an inch in length before catching on something below the skin.

The Dr motioned for Jolien to look into the magnifying lens, as Zahra sat nervously on a laboratory table holding up her shirt to expose her torso. Heisten's basement lab was brightly lit by several rows of overhead lights.

"Do you see how long that thick white hair is? A body hair would be much shorter and would have detached with the tug I just gave it." Bernard commented.

"So what is it?" Jolien queried.

"I suppose this is the question."

Heisten returned to the magnifying lens. The tweezers again grasped the thick white hair. Heisten's tugs made the tiny welt bulge further.

"Does it hurt?" he asked Zahra.

"It just feels like a tiny pinch."

"Ok my dear, we will see about removing this thing, but we need to lance this welt to free it ok?"

Heisten moved to one of the many steel covered tables that ringed the lab, and turned on a Bunsen burner. He then began torching the blade of a utility razor before cleaning the tip with an alcohol wipe. Moving back to Zahra, he gently wiped the welt with alcohol before applying the blade. Careful not to cut the white thread he gently lanced the top of the welt and immediately tugged the white hair free from Zahra's

155

stomach.   Bernard held the tiny hair up to he light and noticed a small object, about half the size of a grain of rice, clinging to the end that had been submerged in Zahra's skin. He quickly moved to another table covered with an assortment of microscopes to examine it. Zahra and Jolien followed him across the room.

The Dr. deposited the hair like object onto an opaque blue slide and pulled the metallurgical stereo zoom microscope toward him. The microscopes incident light flickered on, as Bernard manipulated the course and fine focus adjustments.   He then gently gripped the corners of the slide as he scanned the object under the microscope.

Zahra watched the calculated movements of Bernard Heisten looking for some hint of worry or relief. Heisten turned the nosepiece that held four different objectives of various magnifications, pausing for several long moments at each magnification.

Jolien reminded Heisten of their presence;

"Well what is it?"

Dr. Heisten lifted his head.

"Well it's definitely electronic, and based on the basic design I'd say its some sort of communication device....   Take a look... This is at twenty five" he said as he offered Zahra a peek thought the binocular eye piece.

Zahra leaned into the microscope and saw the head of the device that had been buried in her skin.   It was a razor thin

156

metallic barb with the fine translucent white wire dangling from it.

"This is at one hundred" Bernard declared as he adjusted the nosepiece to the highest magnification. Zahra was now looking at the fine etching of a complex integrated circuit. There appeared to be a maze of precisely assembled conductors running at various levels thought the translucent surface of the object.

"What disturbs me is that consumer electronics this complicated are not being produced at this scale. And yet here it is." Bernard offered in amazement.

Zahra pulled away from the scope to allow Father Jolien a look.

She shared an awkward glance with the doctor, as each pondered the mysterious object that Jolien now examined under the scope.

"What makes you think this thing is a communication device" Jolien questioned still fixated on the magnified image of the object.

"I only guess, at this moment… but from a general design perspective, I am postulating the long hair-like piece is an antenna." Heisten answered.

"An antenna, to receive or to transmit?"

"I think that is good question. One I do not have the answer to… but I would have to say that, regardless, young Zahra here is better off without it in her navel."

"What about this symbol do you think it means anything" Jolien prompted as he handed Heisten the drawing they had traced from the back of the device.

Heisten studied the diagram for a moment.

"And you say this was hidden under the surface eh?"

"Yes it appeared when we rubbed it with our hands" Jolien responded.

"A hidden puzzle this is.. I think we go to the library to find the answer... come. I'll Fi..." He cut himself off, taking stock of the frazzled duo lagging slowly behind him. He continued ahead of them calling for his daughter as he reached the first floor.

"Laura! prepare rooms for our two weary guests" He shouted.

"I will work on this puzzle while you work on recovering your strength." He continued in softer voice directed back at Father Jolien and Zahra.

"Zahra needs to sleep, but I must return to the rectory. There may be some clues there as to the origin of this thing." Father Jolien insisted as he turned to Zahra with a look that seemed to ask if she was ok with his plan.

She considered Heisten's offer for a moment

"I'll be fine here Father... just hurry back.. You're the only one I really trust here."

Jolien kissed her gently on her forehead before hurrying off.

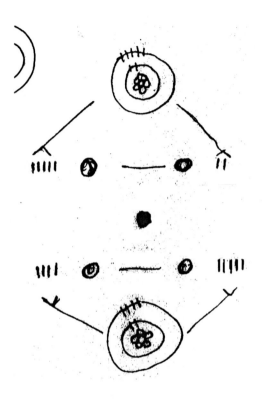

Thick rays of warm daylight traced the center aisle of the old church. They reached down in cones from the cathedral windows. Dust hung motionless, in the air of the old church, glinting in the suns rays. The smell of paraffin and glow of prayer candles from the transepts added to the warm atmosphere of the understated church. An undersized door, off of the vestry, opened to a small study. It was here that the church rector kept a journal of the parish happenings. Births, deaths, tragedies, social concerns, illness, selected sermons, and spiritual writings all of it archived in neat cursive on thick velum. The leather bound journals filled the bookshelves of the study and offered a complete history of the town. Father Jolien sat at the small table flipping though one of the journals, until a torn page caught his eye. The bottom half of the page had been hastily torn from the otherwise well preserved book.

> "There is a strange pall over Mornel this day. Tales of a demon emerging from the night, to feed upon the youngest and purist have been circulating through the town. Only a few profess to have seen the demon, but the story has terrified the entire community. Whispers throughout the Parish tell of Mary of the Needlin family, Gretchen of the Reinhold .."

The Rest of the page was gone.
Jolien followed on the next page.

> "As quickly as the strange menace to our town appeared, it is gone. Like the large majority of the town, no one from the rectory had witnessed the Demon first hand. Tales are being spun of the Lord working through Frank Brein, Christian and David Ferhoff, and Authur Needlin, to rid us of the demon. Beth Needlin was lost in the final encounter with the beast. As was our Sheriff, Frank Brein. Our parishioners, who battled the beast, refused to discuss the final conflict that occurred last night. Perhaps, in time, this journal will include more detail on the challenges faced these last two days.."

Father Jolien jumped from his chair as he felt the hand of Marcus Brein fall upon his shoulder.

"I didn't mean to startle you father"

Father Jolien closed and gathered the journals he had opened into pile as Marcus circled the table.

"I was told you had some information for me?" Marcus sneered.

"I don't think that I do." Jolien offer in a terse response.

"Father, do I detect some anger in your response?"

Father Jolien looked Marcus over as he contemplated a response. After an awkward lag:

"You forget that I hear the confessions of this town Marcus... I hear from young girls, people who steal, corrupt people, a lot of people you might know."

"Some people will say anything Father, especially when it's about a man who might be mayor or this town one day" Marcus reminded Father Jolien, as his hand dropped reflexively to the nickel plated .35 dangling from belt; a convenient resting place for his hand and an instinctive move of intimidation.

"Reading anything good?" Marcus added as he lifted the top journal from the stack. Father Jolien glared at Marcus as he examined the journal.

"You priests keep better records than town hall... I guess until a hundred years ago you WERE town hall, ehh?" Marcus chuckled.

"The good old days." Jolien smirked.

"Yeah this was good year. I think I'll take this one for a little light reading, if you don't mind " Marcus chided as he displayed the journals binding to Father Jolien.

"I wasn't aware you were the type that enjoyed reading." Jolien sneered

"Well I do prefer the movies.. but this is coincidently the same year they have engraved on my grandfather's head stone.

Except that head stone doesn't mean a damn thing anymore since his body just got spit out of the glacier!" Marcus spewed taking note of how his words echoed through the stone chambers.

"That was your grandfather up there?" Jolien asked in a hushed tone.

"Yes ... So why don't you just tell me what you know and save me some trouble?"
Jolien quietly considered his options.

"It doesn't really matter Father, I already have a lead, so I'll find the culprit and whatever it was that was hidden up there."

"You don't scare me son. Your political aspirations won't mean a thing if people start hearing the truth about you... and I am going to make sure they start hearing it. I am an institution in this town son, people trust me, and I am going to make sure people understand that you're not one hundredth the man, or the sheriff, your father was.. or your grandfather was for that matter" the priest retorted.

Marcus surveyed Father Jolien for moment before responding:

"Well I give you that Father, you are quite popular, but I've got a book on everyone of influence in this town. How do you suppose the good God fearing people of our town would react if they found out their trusted Father Jolien was a father in the literal sense?" Marcus smirked as he delivered his threat.

Father Jolien sat stoic at the reading table digesting the fact that Marcus Brein was aware he had sired a child.

"I'm too old to care about what people think of me Marcus, and I was a young man in seminary school, when that happened. It was my first time in the city… I had a lot of questions about what I wanted to do with my life."

"A lot of excuses Father, but to abandon her like that... Her mother turning to prostitution…. Lucky for you she turned out alright… Big fancy author… What was it she wrote?" Marcus sneered.

"Sixty Nine Pathways to the Spirit" Jolien muttered.

"I'd never read that 'new age' crap, Everything I need to know about the spirit is in the good book." as Marcus finished his statement just as the radio on his belt emitted a series of loud beeps. The pattern of beeps evoked a quick response from Marcus. Lifting the radio to his mouth he addressed the dispatcher;

"Brein"

"Sheriff we have an emergency at Reistling's tavern." crackled over the radio static.

"What's the story?" Brein queried.

"Not sure, got eight calls already reporting something 'floating' in. Callers aren't making much sense to be honest." The dispatcher added.

"I'm a just down the street I'll be right there… out" Marcus returned the radio to his

164

belt and handed the journal back to Father Jolien.

"I'll be back Father, and I pray you haven't been holding out on me." Marcus said as he exited the tiny study.

Jolien sat quietly listening to footsteps of Marcus Brein as he ran across the marble flooring of the great church and out the front door.

"I doubt you've ever really prayed for anything Mr. Brein."

Blades of intense sunlight broke through the blinds of the study's picture window, casting uneven stripes of light across the sprawl of books that covered Dr. Heisten's desk. Dr. Heisten leaned over the array of chemistry books, occasionally turning his attention back to the mysterious diagram Zahra and the old priest had sketched for him. He flipped from one diagram of carbon and nitrogen based compounds to the next, waiting for an inspiration that still seemed distant.

The creaking of the study's door signaled his attention to Heidi. She approached in measured steps, balancing a tea cup and saucer in her tiny hands.

"What have you got there?" a smiling Dr. Heisten called across the length of the study to his grand daughter.

"Momma made me hot chocolate, but this is not hot chocolate." Heidi stated with seriousness that made the doctor chuckle.

"That's right, it is tea I believe.." He noted.

"Momma says to tell you to take a break." She stated continuing her mission with the same seriousness.

Dr. Heisten quickly cleared a corner of the desk to receive Heidi's offering.

"For you I will take a break." Heisten declared taking Heidi into his arms the moment she released the tea cup. Heidi giggled as the doctor tickled her ribs.

"What are you doing poppa?"

"I'm trying to figure out a puzzle." He stated.

"Where's a puzzle?" a confused Heidi asked as she scanned the sprawl of books.

"It's not a picture puzzle like you are used to. It's a puzzle about elements and chemicals." He explained.

"What's a element?" Heidi asked.

"Well, they are like things you can mix together and make bigger things with….. Kind of like your mom mixing chocolate powder and milk to make hot chocolate." The Dr. clarified.

"Momma didn't use milk.. Momma got bad milk by accident." Heidi noted.

"The milk was spoiled?" Heisten tried to coax from his grand daughter.

"No it had hor-worms.. Momma doesn't like hor-worms." She corrected.

"Hormones." The doctor corrected Heidi's pronunciation. "Your mother likes organic food."

"What's organic?" Heidi queried.

"It means the farmer does not use chemicals and hormones or genetically alter or.." Heisten paused as the structure of four genetic compounds flashed through his brain.

"Yeah, momma doesn't like that stuff so she just added water." Heidi added filling Dr. Heisten's silence.

"Thank you Heidi. I think you just helped me solve a puzzle." The doctors proclaimed, as he pulled his grand daughter toward the book shelves. The confused young girl stared up at her grandfather, as his fingers traced the spines of the wall of books.

"Genetics, genetics, genetics.." he mumbled.

"Here it is 575." He declared removing a book titled "Genetic Sequencing"

Heidi continued her confused stare as he fanned through the book.

Dr. Heisten paused on a series of diagrams at the books center.

"I think we got it." Dr Hesisten stated with a confident smile in Heidi's direction.

Heidi smiled back up at him with the same excited smile.

As Marcus approached the Reistling tavern he could see the wait staff and twenty or so spectators standing across the street and staring in through the open front door. Transfixed by what they saw inside, no one noticed Marcus approaching the pub until he was nearly in the doorway. He popped the leather holster strap that retained his .35, as he peered around the front door jam.

The tavern was a mess. It appeared as if everyone had fled in a great hurry. Chairs lay fallen on their back, drinks were spilled on almost every table, and full serving trays had been dropped in the aisles. It was a scene made surreal by the upbeat melodic thumping of polka music playing over the sound system.

In contrast to the music, Marcus moved slowly and deliberately with his gun now drawn. He could see no one, nor any "floating" object, in the main dining area. To his left was a small hallway that led to the kitchen and across the room to his right was a staircase to an outdoor patio. From behind him, across the street, he heard one of the wait staff yell out: "It went in the kitchen".

He approached the hallway entrance slowly leveling his gun in front of him with two hands. As the hallway revealed itself, he spotted Adeline lying unconscious on the floor. She lay with her head in the junction of two doorways: one to the kitchen the other to a staircase that spiraled to the basement. Marcus approached her only to be startled by the levitating device as it emerged from the basement stairwell. Marcus crept back slowly keeping his sidearm trained on the device. The device turned toward Marcus hovering over Adeline's prostrate body, and paused for moment before moving toward him.

Marcus backed himself to the edge of a table in the main dining area as the device continued to levitate in his direction. His finger tightened on the trigger as the device closed the distance between them to a meter. Then, the device stopped. Marcus contemplated his next move as the device hovered silently in front of him.

The instant the laser light sprayed toward Marcus his finger squeezed the trigger, and the tavern erupted in noise and flashing light. Marcus dodged toward the front door as his .35 discharged its fourth round. The bullets ticked off the metal skin of the device leaving only tiny sparks and the sound of ricochet. From outside the screams of terrified and now scattering onlookers filtered through the doorway. The device rose and took a trajectory toward the staircase to the outdoor patio. The gun boomed twice more as the device fled up the staircase, then only the click of the hammer slapping against the empty chamber. Marcus gave chase, but could only watch as the device flew off the outdoor patio and into the distance.

Marcus made his way back down the stairs and returned his attention, once again, to the unconscious Adeline. The old Priest's words rung through his head again: "I hear the confessions of this town, young girls.."

Marcus had suspected Adeline could not keep a secret, and his blood boiled at the thought of her confiding in Father Jolien. "Maybe it was one of the earlier girls" he thought. "No, she's a talker", he concluded. Marcus glanced through the front door, and noted the spectators had fled at the sound of gunfire. He also noted that the hallway where Adeline lay was not visible from the street. He nonchalantly lifted a small stack of napkins, from a serving station, as he approached Adeline in calculated steps. He paused for a moment standing above her. Adeline had dropped on her back, her hands raised just above her shoulders. Even as his heart pounded through his chest, Marcus coolly dropped a cloth napkin on each of her forearms. Standing to the left of her torso: he dropped his shin down onto her right forearm, and leaned across her body to hold the other forearm down with one hand. The napkins shielded her delicate skin from bruising under the weight of his shin and the tightness of his grip. His free left hand clenched a final napkin. He held it for moment, feeling his adrenaline rush. His pulse was visible in the veins of his neck, and pounding in his ears. With a scrowl he began to stuff the napkin into Adeline's mouth. With half of the thick cloth inserted in her mouth, Marcus then placed his large

170

callused hand down over Adeline's mouth and nose. Her small delicate face was nearly covered by Marcus's hand.

Nothing happened for a moment as Marcus turned away from Adeline's face to keep an eye, and ear, on anyone coming into the dining area through the front door. He had to listen carefully over the festive music still booming from the jukebox. After ten seconds, Adeline's unconscious brain was alarmed to the lack of oxygen. Marcus watched calmly as her legs convulsed in an attempt to free herself from his grip, her hand clutching and tugging at his pant leg. A few more seconds and Adeline's body stopped moving. Marcus remained in position calmly waiting. He had never taken it this far, he was afraid he'd enjoy it, and he had been right. Another minute passed before a final leg twitch seemed to signal something to Marcus.

He loosened his grip on Adeline and removed the napkin from her mouth stuffing it in his jacket pocket. He gathered the other two napkins and threw them to the side. Marcus heard footsteps entering the dining area. He leaned his ear down over Adeline's mouth and turned his head to look down her torso.

Deputy Weiss entered the hallway to see Marcus pretending to check Adeline's vital signs.

"What the hells go'n on Marcus?"

"She's dead." Marcus stated flatly.

"Did you do CPR?"

"For the last five minutes.. " Marcus returned with a false sigh of disappointment.

"No help... she's dead"

"Who the hell killed her?"

"WHAT the hell killed her.. I don't know what it was... It flew up to the patio... Check if it's still there.." Marcus commanded.

Weiss pointed himself toward the staircase across the tavern with his gun drawn. Marcus watched as Weiss began to ascend the staircase.

Marcus placed his mouth over Adeline's, and ran his tongue across her purple and motionless lips. He had to sell this CPR story now. He then shifted his attention to Adeline's torso, locking his hands together in ball between her breasts.

"Sorry dear, we're gonna have to crack your sternum." He whispered before forcing his fists downward into Adeline's chest. A muffled cracking sound emitted from her lifeless body.

The smell of the down comforter and the soft mattress convinced Zahra that it had all been a dream. She was home in her own bed, she was sure of it; until she felt the gently nudges of Milo kneading the comforter over her chest. As her mind recounted the events of the prior two days her eyelids slowly opened. The late afternoon sun was muted by the heavy red fabric that draped the windows. However, there was enough light to confirm she was not at home. Zahra sat up in the bed and scratched Milo between his ears as he continued nuzzling her chest. Her hand felt a hairless patch on the back of Milo's neck centered by a tiny circular bandage. Milo flinched as she touched the bandage, then scurried away.

It was then that her glaze fell upon young Heidi, as she stood clutching a stuffed animal. Zahra's amputated calf protruded from the comforter. It was swollen, blistered, and resting on a towel blotted with tiny bloodstains. Heidi was examining the stump until its movement alerted her to Zahra's consciousness.

"Hello little girl." Zahra whispered as she fought off a yawn.

Heidi moved back timorously, as Zahra noticed her exposed stump.

"I'm sorry this is pretty gross huh?" Zahra asked referring to her blistered stump.

Heidi was still frozen and speechless.

"It's not as bad as it looks." Zahra reassured as she wrapped the blistered stump in the towel, and hid it under the sheets.

Heidi took advantage of Zahra's focus on covering her leg to flee the room.

Zahra had become used to the reaction of children to her injury. She did not hold Heidi's reaction against her. There had been many occasions, especially early in her injury, where she had to remove her prosthetic in the presence of children. Zahra felt awake and rested as she sat in the bed stretching her neck and arms.

Father Jolien entered the room as Zahra was reaching to the side of the bed for her prosthetic.

"Sleep well?" he asked.

"Yeah, pretty good actually." Zahra noted.

"Do you need anything for the leg?" Jolien offered as he noticed Zahra's blistered stump, which was again exposed.

"You wear that prosthetic enough and you can't even feel the blisters. One thing that bothers me is that doctors always call it a residual limb? When I think of residual, or residue, I think of something you didn't want to leave behind but couldn't get off… ya-know? Residue! It's the stuff that's caked to the sides of an empty soup bowl… It's like saying we really didn't want to leave you any limb at all but that piece just wouldn't come off." Zahra finished with a chuckle.

"You'd think they could come up with something more.... I don't know ... Positive sounding..... Like Persistent limb...salvaged limb.." Jolien suggested, as he stood at the foot of the bed.

"Post amputive limb. These names are getting too long. How 'bout we just cut the 'g' off and call it a 'le'..." dead-panned Zahra, before breaking into a wide smile.

The priest chuckled along with her.

"What time is it?" Zahra queried, wiping the crust from her eyes.

"It's late afternoon, You slept for a long time.... I just got back... I ran into your old buddy Sheriff Brein."

"How does a guy like that stay sheriff?" she exhaled.

"Well he barely won the last election. He started some rumors about the good man who was running against him two years ago, a real sleazy campaign....... I am going to make sure he looses the next one." the old priest promised.

"What did he want with you?"

"Information from the parish archives. His grandfather died trying to destroy that thing seventy years ago. The body just came out of the glacier. Marcus is an even angrier man these days."

"Does he know it was me.. who dug it up?" Zahra asked.

"He mentioned he had a lead, but he left before I could press him for details. I think whatever that thing was, it was floating

176

around town today." the priest noted somberly.

Zahra thought quietly for a moment.

"Where's Dr Heisten?" she asked.

"In the Lab, according to Laura.... He asked that we join him when you awoke." Jolien answered.

A muffled response to their calls seemed to be coming from a basement door. Zahra followed the winding stairs down to the same basement lab she and Jolien had visited earlier.

They found Dr Heisten busy at a lab table covered with flasks, test tubes, bunsen burners, graduated cylinders and other chemistry paraphernalia.

"Dr Heisten, what is all this?" she asked.

"You call me Bernard, please. This is the answer to a puzzle... I'll explain"

Bernard moved to one of the white boards that lined the laboratory walls.

"There are four nitrogenous bases that combine to form DNA... " Bernard began drawing diagrams or chemical compounds calling out each ones name as he finished.

"Thymine..... Cytosine .... Adenine........ Guanine"

Bernard stepped back from the board.

"Now, what do you see at the center of all those diagrams?" Bernard asked.

Jolien and Zahra examined each diagram. At the center of each was a ring shaped structure of Carbon and Nitrogen atoms.

"Carbon and Nitrogen" Zahra made the connection before the priest.

"Very good... Also notice the number of carbon and nitrogen atoms varies in each compound. Let's look at the puzzle again." Bernard drew the puzzle on the white board.

"See the line joining the bottom dots and the line joining the upper dots?... When DNA is formed these four chemicals pair to each other, these pairs are called base pairs. Adenine always pairs with Thymine, and Guanine always pairs with Cytosine.... These bonds are what I believe these two horizontal lines represent." Bernard was on a roll as Jolien and Zahra struggled to follow along.

"So if the top and bottom dots are each a pair... Thymine and Adenine contain the same number of carbon atoms, so they must be the lower two on the diagram.. differentiated by the number of carbon atoms you see? Are you understanding this?" Bernard watched as the two studied the increasingly complex diagrams on the white board. He continued in the hope his explanation would become clear.

"The other pair, Cytosine and Guanine can be differentiated by the number or nitrogen they contain. They are the top pair, do you see on the diagram? "Bernard recognized the confusion in Jolien but could see that Zahra was beginning to understand.

"Four carbons in Cytosine.. Five carbons in Guanine... Two Nitrogen in Thymine.... Five nitrogen in Adenine..." Zahra stated her understanding of the puzzle.

"Precisely." Heisten affirmed as he turned to the priest for a hint of understanding that did not come. "Well the chemical structure is of little consequence; perhaps I am clouding this with too much detail. Just under stand that the four dots represent the four basic components that make up DNA."

"I think I got that... But what is the center dot for?" Jolien queried.

"Ah! Good question, when you remove Nitrogen and Carbon from these compounds what you are left with?"

Zahra's eyes scanned the diagrams "H..... and O.... Hydrogen and Oxygen"

"And what can we make from that?" Heisten prodded.

"Water?" Jolien stated hesitantly.

"Yes, there are a few things that can be made from hydrogen and Oxygen; but given the context of this puzzle, and the fact that most living things contain a high percentage of H_2O, water would be the best guess.... Now some of these bases are not fluid in their pure form, so what I am doing is separating the bases from organic material, and preparing a solution with distilled water." Heisten explained.

The three paused as Milo scurried down the basement stairs and across the lab before disappearing behind a cabinet.

"I'm impressed Dr Heisten, but what about the thing that was stuck in my stomach?" Zahra asked.

"Looks like Milo came just on cue...... I surmised if it was a transmitter it was probably leaching electrical energy from the nervous system" Heisten answered as he leaned down to retrieve Milo from behind the cabinet.

Father Jolien stepped over to assist the doctor as he continued his explanation.

"So, I used Milo as a host for it.. just a tiny incision on his back." Heisten continued.

Zahra noticed Father Jolien tapping on the back of the crouching Dr Heisten, and turned her attention to him. A strange look was coming over Jolien's face.

"I think you were right." Jolien muttered.

"How do you know?" Followed Zahra, finally noticing that Father Jolien was looking directly over her shoulder at the staircase.

"Because it found us." Jolien finished, as he raised his finger and pointed to the device. It levitated less than a meter behind Zahra.

Just a few hundred meters outside the Heisten compound, the thick plank door of the old feed house slowly creaked open. Marcus Brein entered the Zahra's registered lodging. His eyes scanned the empty room as he made his way to the center. Removing his leather gloves Marcus touched the wood stove tentatively at first then pressing his whole palm against the top of the iron stove. It was cold; no one had been there for a long while. Marcus walked around the living space looking for some sign of the Zahra or the device. Nothing seemed to draw his attention until he spotted Zahra's sketchbook, as it sat on the dining table. Marcus strolled over to the small square table and flipped the sketchbook open. His fingers fanned the pages open one by one until he spotted Zahra's rendering of the device. He was in the right place.

IX: Genetics & Evolution

Zahra jumped to the side and allowed the device to approach Bernard Heisten.

"Zahra, close the door behind you." Heisten whispered as if noise would somehow either scare or attract the device.

"Zahra leave.... Go upstairs." Jolien commanded in the same hushed tone.

Zahra, still nervous from her prior encounter, made no argument as she cautiously sidestepped her way to the stair well.

Father Jolien locked the laboratory door behind her. Bernard removed the leather belt from his trousers, as the device angled toward the metal cabinet that Milo had disappeared behind. Jolien followed Dr Heisten's lead and removed his belt as well, as both men edged their way to the rear of the device. Bernard wrapped his leather belt around the base of the device and fastened the buckle at its widest eyelet. He then motioned for Father Jolien's belt as the device continued to hold it position in front of the cabinets. Receiving the priest's belt, he linked it through his own, and around the leg of a nearby lab table.

The device was anchored now to the heavy metal lab table, by the two-link leather chain.

"I had a thought that the transmitter we pulled from Zahra might be powered by the electrical pulses that run through our bodies." Bernard repeated in a whisper. "So, I inserted it under the skin of Milo... Amazing that it actually worked."

Bernard opened a plastic container on the lab table and removed a handful of disposable syringes. His hands working fast and deliberate as he alternately glanced over at the device. Theoren Jolien watched silently as Bernard prepared five syringes, filling them from the beakers on the table. The device seemed content to hover directly in front of the metal cabinet. Heisten made mental note of the contents of each syringe and placed them in order between the fingers of his left hand. Each gap between his fingers filled, he held the fifth and final syringe between his teeth. The doctor then turned his full attention to the device. His eyes scanned the surface of what appeared to be the devices dorsal. Jolien recognized what he was looking for and pointed the general area he had seen the puzzle appear.

He rubbed gently the spot Jolien had pointed out. The puzzle appeared just as they had drawn it. Bernard soon located the five tiny pinholes that had been described. Heisten removed the syringe he had filled with distilled water from his teeth, and injected it slowly into the middle hole of the diagram. The device remained motionless, as Bernard tossed the emptied syringe indiscriminately onto the table. Bernard raised a syringe he had filed with a Guanine solution and injected it in the appropriate

185

hole.   The Device suddenly lowered to the ground and came to rest. Startled, the priest and Bernard both stepped back from the device, before cautiously approaching once again.   Milo jumped out from behind the cabinet onto the largest of the laboratory tables. He scurried across it hugging the wall, and nearly tipping some flasks, as he moved across the lab.

"Grab   him"   Bernard   directed   Jolien motioning to Milo as he cowered in the back corner of the lab table. Jolien had to move quickly to grab the jittery cat, and he winced in pain as Milo dug his claws into his chest.

"Take him upstairs… I think it's safe if Zahra wants to come down… It appears to be shutdown" Bernard suggested in a tone now less hushed.

Jolien   silently   followed   Bernard's instruction, closing the door behind him as he exited the lab.   Heisten continued the process of injecting the nitrogenous bases into their respective holes. Bernard emptied his final syringe and stepped back waiting for something to happen. A small pop was heard as the device split open symmetrically along its dorsal. The sides slowly parted to reveal an elaborate tapestry of wires, tubes, hydraulic pistons, and supporting struts. The finger like protrusion that topped the device spit open as well, and at the same time lifted upward. The sphere that centered the device cracked open along its equator and the top lifted in concert with the raising finger like protrusion.   Inside the sphere, a collection of spinning discs were slowly coming to a stop, like the stacked platters of a large hard drive.

In the top platter a circular platform that remained stationary held a translucent green disk, above which a needle like probe hung. Bernard realized he was looking at something far more technically advanced then he'd ever seen. When the outer skin had fully exploded, a holographic image appeared above the "eye" of the device.

Bernard gingerly grabbed the device by the now exploded panels, and positioned it in the middle of the open space that centered the lab. The device now faced the stairwell, still chained by the leather belts to the table behind it.   The hologram now floated in the very center of the lab. Bernard examined holographic symbols that hovered over the device.   In the center floated two equilateral triangles one pointing up the other down. Beneath the triangles, hung an animated 3D model of the device closing its shell, disappearing, and then reappearing in its open state. To the upper left of center hovered a 3D double helix that alternately morphed into a branch diagram of circles and lines.   To the upper right cycled spinning models of three different objects; one of which was the device itself, another resembled a pill shaped metal container, and the last appeared to be an octagonal sail with cylinders mounted at the joints.   Bernard surmised that touching the lowest icon would close the device, and he could not yet figure out what the right most icon was trying to illustrate. He reached his hand out and touched the floating double helix. Since it was DNA that had gotten him this far, he decided that is where he should start.   Upon touching the helix the icons shifted; the center triangles dropped to the lower right and the upward pointing triangle began blinking bright purple. The remaining icons shrank and shifted to the same, albeit smaller, configuration to the lower left.   In the wide space where the icons originally sat there was nothing.   Bernard contemplated whether or not to touch the blinking purple triangle. After a moment, he decided it was the logical next step.   Bernard was slowly reaching for the upward pointing triangle when a he was startled by a voice that seemed to emanate from the device.

"Father!"

"I'm glad you could make it." offered Deputy Weiss as he stood over Adeline's lifeless body. Father Jolien shook his head at the injustice of a dead teenager. No matter how many of these rites he had performed, the young ones always left a particularly bitter taste.

"How did she die?"

188

"We don't know. This thing just came out of nowhere and she was dead." Weiss explained.

Father Jolien thought for a moment how convenient this was for Marcus Brein. The girl who had confessed to him so many horrible stories involving the town's sheriff now lay dead at his feet.

"Thing?" Jolien queried as he knelt down beside Adeline's body.

"Yeah, some floating metal....thing. I didn't see it myself but that's the reports we're getting." Weiss reported.

"So you didn't see her die?"

"No, Marcus was the first one on the scene." Weiss responded.

"Where's Marcus now?"

"Don't know. He ran off after whatever it was that killed her... You need him for something?" asked a perplexed deputy Weiss.

"No, just trying to sort things out.... May I close her eyes?" asked Jolien after kissing the end of his stole.

"Sure Father, I don't see the harm. M.E. and the photographer already had their look." Weiss watched quietly as Father Jolien finish his prayer and gently closed Adeline's eyelids.

"She reminds me of my daughter." Jolien stated flatly to a surprised deputy Weiss.

"Your daughter??"

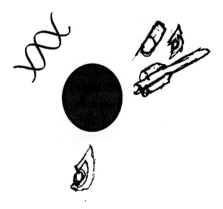

Bernard had recoiled at the word "father". In the empty basement lab, the purple triangle was still blinking. It took several seconds for Bernard to recognize his daughter Laura's voice emanating from an intercom mounted to the wall behind the device. She had beckoned him to come upstairs to the kitchen,

Now Bernard Heisten found himself sitting dumbfounded at the kitchen table with Zahra and his daughter. Father Jolien had left to investigate Laura's story.

A story he could not believe.

"I just can't believe it would kill like that.. are you certain?" He questioned.

"Yes! I am telling you that device you have killed a girl in town." Laura exclaimed.

"And you say you heard this from three separate people?" Zahra chimed in.

"Yes!"

"And they're saying it just touched her and she died." Zahra followed.

"That's what they're saying! We have to call the police." Laura retorted as she approached the wall mounted phone.

"NO!" Bernard shouted as he stood up to approach his daughter.

"Maybe this girl died of shock or something.. Maybe she fainted and hit her head... but the device seems to be shut down now, and I will need a few hours or so to figure out what it is." Bernard declared.

"Father this was a healthy teenage girl that died. I don't think it was an accident." Laura protested.

"You should not be caught up in this... take Heidi and get on the train home tonight. " Bernard insisted.

"I don't want to leave you here with some weird.... thing, and some strangers." Laura persisted.

"Do not worry about me, my dear. You look after Heidi... Go collect your things .. There is a nine thirty train to catch." Heisten insisted as he ushered Laura out of the kitchen.

"Perhaps you'd like to stay at my little chalet? It's not far." Zahra suggested.

"Yes this is a good idea!... They have the old rustic feed house just down the mountain from us.... It will be like camping for you and Heidi." Bernard added excitedly.

"At some point I was going to retrieve my sketch pad.... I can show you down and get the place heated up.." Zahra offered.

Laura was hesitant to accept this solution to her fear of the device, but she trusted her father implicitly. His insistence wore her down and she found herself packing an overnight bag for herself and Heidi.

Bernard and Zahra returned to the basement lab, relieved to find the device in the condition Dr. Heisten had left it. The translucent purple triangle still glowed brighter every few seconds. Bernard took a minute to explain the brief interaction he had had with the device when Zahra had left, and his belief that the triangle was asking to be touched. Zahra nodded and waited with bated breath as Bernard hit the triangle. A three dimensional model of a pill shaped metallic container appeared just above the device's eye. In the center of the field a tiny white dot appeared, and the pill shaped container emitted tiny bursts of white gas. The pill seemed to be reorientating itself to point lengthwise toward the glowing white dot. The pill then split in two emitting a bright blue glow as the front half of the pill thrust toward the white dot. The back half of the pill disappeared, reminding Dr Heisten of a disposable rocket stage. The front half of the pill continued to emit a blue flame as the white dot began to grow. As it grew, details began to emerge. The dot soon formed a white cloud. Bernard turned out the lights in the lab to see the translucent animation more clearly. As the white cloud dispersed, galaxies began to appear. Bernard recognized the illustration was showing the, now thimble shaped, container traveling inward toward the center of the universe. Something bothered Bernard though; the animation started with the entire universe appearing as a dot of light from the pill shaped objects perspective. How could something have gotten that far out? It seemed it would have traveled further than the light emitted during the birth of the

194

universe. He wished he could replay the animation, just as he noticed the purple triangles that had dropped to the lower right now both glow a bright purple. On a hunch, he touched the downward pointing triangle and the animation froze. He glanced over at Zahra with a smile on his face.

"Just like a VCR." Bernard chuckled, before hitting the downward triangle again to reverse the animation. He let it reverse at double speed until it had reached the beginning, then touched the upward pointing triangle to play the animation again. Bernard was convinced it was showing the pill shaped container far on the outskirts of the universe. He watched as the animation continued past the point he had rewound from. The device shot toward a cluster of stars in the center of a dense galaxy. The blue light faded as the container seemed to be zeroed in on a single star now. He had not recognized the galaxy from the angle it approached but he soon recognized the solar system the thimble shaped container was rocketing toward.

"That's us.. That's our system." Bernard exclaimed.

The vessel in the animation re-orientated itself, spinning 180 degrees. The open side now faced forward. Another burst of blue light slowed it, before the nose cone of the container detached and fanned open to reveal a representation of the very device that stood before them. The device

195

detached from the shell it had been encased in and took aim at a blue planet.

"That does not look like us." Zahra did not recognize the land formations coming into detail on the blue planet.

"This is the ancient world... The surface rides on a mantle of liquid rock. Plate tectonics shifted the planet into its current configuration." Bernard explained quickly not taking his eyes off the animation.

The animation showed the device glowing fiery red as it entered the atmosphere. It plunged into the ocean with a hissing, steaming, splash.

The device emerged from the ocean and began moving toward a brown patch on the horizon. Upon reaching the pebble covered beach the device stopped and rotated 360 degrees. After a moment, the device turned abruptly, and moved left along the waters edge. It stopped again and angled downward toward the rolling surf. The animation showed the violet beam that had emitted from the actual device. The device seemed to be scanning something at the water's edge. The land, the ocean, the device, and everything else in the animation began to fade. From the spot at the waters edge the model of a strange fish began to grow and move to the center of the holograms field. Soon only the fish remained in hologram.

"What is that? It looks half lizard, half fish." Zahra muttered.

"It's Dipterus... and extinct lungfish.." Heisten replied still focused on the hologram.

To the fish's left a long multi-colored double helix appeared. Two short double helix diagrams appeared even further left and then merged into the longer double helix string. The Lungfish changed appearance and became even more reptilian. Again two small double helix illustrations appeared and merged into the longer string. The Hologram showed what appeared to be a primitive lizard now.

"It's showing us evolution?" Bernard muttered only half aware he had asked the question aloud. Each time a snippet of genetic code appeared to the far left and merged with the long double helix the holographic animal changed its characteristics.

Bernard suddenly had the idea to speed the animation up. He pressed the upward triangle twice more, and the animation seemed to morph before his eyes. The segments of genetic code appeared and merged into the double helix at a dizzying pace. The two spectators watched in amazement as the reptilian hologram transformed in to hairy rodent like animal. Then it grew in size, as it transformed into a lemur like creature. The lemur slowly grew and morphed into a strange looking primate. Continuing at a hurried pace the double helix diagram had grown in length, and separated into two strands. An early humanoid appeared who then morphed into Neanderthals becoming more human with each passing second.

"They are all female these images." Bernard noted as the progression continued.

After a few more seconds clothing began to adorn the images simple wraps made from animal hair at first then becoming more complex as the form of modern humans emerged.

"Wait!" Bernard exclaimed, reaching for the downward pointing triangle and tapping it twice. The dizzying motion of the hologram suddenly stopped. The hologram displayed a wide-eyed young woman wearing a simple red dirndl. Her hair was braided and twisted into a ball on the back of her head.

"She looks familiar too." Bernard muttered, before hitting the downward triangle to reverse the animation. After backing up six images Bernard stopped the animation. A young woman of supple features appeared. A long blue veil with white trim covered her head and draped down over her bosom.

"Do you recognize this girl?" Bernard queried.

"Mother of God…" muttered Zahra

An oil painting of the Holy Mother, done in the classic style, hung in the private study of Theoren Jolien. She had soft features and wisps of brown hair protruded from underneath the shroud of blue and white.

Father Jolien sat in a leather chair, a wooden box on his lap. In his hand he held a book. The wooden box held a jumble of photographs and mementos from his past. He thought back to when he was a young man of eighteen, and attending seminary school. Aida was a seamstress working in her fathers tailor shop. He had entered on a Saturday, and Aida's father was busy tending to an important and wealthy client. Her father had asked Aida to "measure this young man". Having lived his adolescence between the rectory in Mornel and the Seminary school in Bern; Theoren Jolien was unaccustomed to the touch of a woman. He felt the tinge of chemical attraction as her thin warm hand took his. She guided him over to a thick wooden box, upon which he was supposed to step up. Aida had long curly black hair that she wore in single thick braid down the center of her back. Her hair contrasted the smooth light skin of her face. Theoren found he could only glance at her for moment before looking away. His face felt flush. Jolien looked down as Aida leaned into him, reaching around his waist with the tape measure, her breasts brushed against his abdomen. Theoren felt himself becoming aroused, as he peered down the open top of Aida loosely fitting blouse. Jolien was being measured for a new frock the seminary had commissioned. Only his height, waist, and shoulder measurements were of any consequence. Aida was unaware or this and was running the full battery of measurements. Aida's hand pressed the tape measure against Theorens inseam and began streaming its way up his inner thigh. Jolien stared at the ceiling, as it was becoming apparent from Aida's quiet giggle, that his loose fitting trousers were not doing anything to harness his rising…. excitement.

Hearing his daughter's giggle, Aida's father asked sternly;

"What's the matter over there?"

Jolien was thankful that he was facing away from the senior tailor.

"Nothing father" Aida replied. As Jolien glanced down, he found her smiling wryly up at him. Aida scribbled on a small pad before walking away. Theoren remained on the box praying that his hormonal outburst would miraculously subside, so he could exit the shop without further embarrassment, or the wrath of a man who made his living with scissors. Aida returned a moment later with Theoren's coat in her hand.

"I thought you might need this" she offered with a wink.

Jolien folded the coat over his forearm and held it against his waist. The thick jacket draped over his groin to conceal his… indiscretion. He made a hasty exit from the store, his face red with embarrassment.

200

A few days later the young Jolien came back to pick up his frock.   He found the store empty but for the nineteen year old Aida. She flashed a flirtatious smile as he entered, and Theoren found his face blushing again.

"I'm here to pick up a white surplice" Theoren stammered.

"What's a surplice?" Aida asked coyly.

"It's like a gown."

Aida nodded before asking: "You're from the seminary, aren't you?"

As he looked at Aida, Theoren was wishing more and more that he was not.

"Yes" reluctantly escaped Theoren's lips.

"What's your name?" Aida asked.

"Theoren Jolien"

Aida considered it for a moment.

"That's a nice name….. Come with me, we'll find your surplus."

"That's surplice." Jolien corrected.

"Yeah, right." Aida said as she moved from the counter to the racks of clothes that extended out from back wall of the tailor shop.

Theoren followed her as she moved down the first row of garments looking at tags attached to the hangers.

"You know, you're not the first to have that happen" Aida slyly noted.

"I'm sorry about that.." Jolien stammered apologetically, his face reddening once again.

"You don't have to be sorry..   It's a natural thing… It doesn't bother me"

Theoren felt mildly relieved at her acceptance but was uncomfortable with the entire topic of sex.

"If you were one of the fat old perverts who come in here, I'd mind…. but you're cute." Aida continued to flirt with Theoren.

Theoren was at a lost as to how to handle the situation he was in. He had never before been the object of a girl's desire.

Aida was enjoying the power she had over Theoren. In her prior relationships with boys, she had always been the less experienced. She felt in control with Theoren and it sparked an agression in her she would normally not display.

"So you are going to be priest?"

"Yes" Theoren muttered, wishing with each glance at Aida's curves that it were not so.

"And that means you can't have sex right?"

"Yes.. I suppose it does."

"Have you ever?" she asked, as she turned to look Theoren directly in the eyes.

Theoren turned away from her glance, as he muttered a sheepish "No"

"How can you be sure it's something you want to give up?" she said, pulling a clean white gown from the rack.

Theoren had no response as the two looked at each other in an awkward silence.

"Wouldn't you like to at least know what it's like to kiss a girl?" she added with a sly grin, as she moved closer to Theoren.

She held the gown to his chest, and looked at him yearningly.

Before Theoren Jolien knew it his hands were cradling her delicate jaw line, and his lips were pressed against hers. He let her guide his movements with the hand she place on the back of his head. Her soft tongue entered his mouth and he returned its playful jabs with his own. Slowly, she peeled away from his kiss.

"You seem to have found some control for you little friend" Aida nonchalantly commented.

"I'm just wearing tighter underwear." Theoren confessed.

Over fifty years had passed since that encounter and it was still burned in Theoren's mind. Burned as well was the memory of the evening Father Xavier investigated a strange moaning noise emanating from the scriptorium, and entered to find his prized pupil fornicating with a young seamstress. Theoren had desecrated holy space. He left that night on his own volition. Two months later he found himself two hundred miles away, in the small town of Findlehof. He had been living in railroad cars for nearly two weeks. It was in Findlehof that he entered a small wooden church, and found the confessional. Theoren confessed all that had transpired as tears streamed down his face. The shadowy figure in the confessional introduced himself as Father Huen. He took pity on Theoren, and after a few days of politicking on his behalf,

Father Huen offered him the chance to return to another seminary, where he could begin his studies anew.

Theoren was unaware of Aida's pregnancy until he returned seven years later. Theoren had stayed away from Bern intentionally. He wanted no further temptations until he had completed his journey to priesthood. His relationship with Aida had lasted only a month, but it had been enough for Theoren to reconsider his direction in life. Several times since he had thoughts of quitting the seminary, and always a life with Aida flashed though his mind. Everything about her was contradictory to what he had studied about virtue and chastity, but when he recalled his tender moments with her he only felt love. Shortly after his ordainment Theoren found himself traveling through Bern.

Theoren buttoned his overcoat to the top button, and wrapped his scarf around his neck, as he approached the tailor shop. Partly to shield himself from the chilling breeze, but also to completely cover his cassock. He intended a dramatic unveiling to surprise Aida with the status of his priesthood.

Aida's father still bore the same serious look as Theoren inquired about her whereabouts. Theoren was shocked at the terse response he received from him:

"I haven't seen that little slut in five years... got herself knocked up, gotta be ahhh.. seven years ago now... Does she owe you something?"

"No" was the only word a shocked Theoren could find.

"Oh you must be from the orphanage?... Cause Ingrid is not with me anymore she's with my sister in Brig."

"Ingrid?" a light headed Theoren muttered.

"Aida's kid.. Ingrid"

"Oh yes.. where is she?"

"You should get you records straight down there." Aida's father sneered, as he took a notepad from his front pocket and began scribbling an address.

"What about the father?" Theoren asked hesitantly.

"Someone told me at the time they had seen her run'n about with a seminary boy.. She never would say who it was... and believe you me, I tried to belt it out of her... could have been anyone with the way she flirted about.. "

Theoren clenched his jaw and adjusted his scarf to make sure his collar was covered.

"You don't have to worry though, my sister's family is a good home."

Theoren questioned the endorsement of a home, from a man who had just called his daughter a slut and admitted to beating her. Theoren excused himself politely as a palpable wave of guilt ran down his body.

Several days later Theoren was posted outside a school house in Brig waiting for the recess bell to ring. When the doors opened and the children filed out, Theoren caught a glimpse of a face undeniably similar to his own. He approached the young girl who bore his features and asked her for a name. She responded "Ingrid Nea... sorry my new name is Ingrid Wells now"

Theoren was immediately aware that he was in fact a father.

Theoren Jolien returned to Mornel and watched from afar as his daughter grew up. He had the local pastor in Brig update him regularly. He would periodically mail her money anonymously.

Theoren Jolien stared at the cover of the book.

"69 Paths to the Spirit.

By Ingrid Wells"

The book postulated that the spirit sat above conscious thought, and as information passed from the primitive brain to the limbic and then neocortex it stepped through opposing binary paths. Sensory input was broken into pleasure and pain in the primitive brain, and then branched to the emotional registers of pride or shame within the limbic layer. The neocortex then divided the input into fear and desire. Thus a three digit binary system had eight possible paths to the spirit. Outbound information was passed in a similar fashion, taking the path of trust or doubt at the neocortex. Then love and anger at the limbic layer, and ending with a choice to act or ignore at primitive brain. With three layers, and two choices at each, there were again eight possible paths for outbound signals. With eight in, and eight out, there were thus 64 paths through the spirit that passed through the lower brain. The book further postulated that one could achieve a meditative state whereby the spirit could signal directly to the five sensory inputs, bypassing lower brain pathways. Sixty nine paths.

He opened the book to the inside of the back cover. The inside of the jacket included a photo of his daughter at forty. She was dressed in a smart but plain sweater, and seemed to radiate kindness and understanding with her soft smile and earthy appearance. She had written a book that examined the very nature of spiritual thought.

Father Jolien was proud of his daughter.

XI : Epistemology

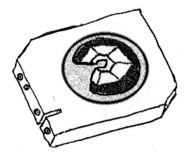

"Geoffrey, what the hell are we doing up here?" Officer Reinhold moaned as the red tinted binoculars fell from his face.

"You're spotting for me." Deputy Weiss responded, as he continued to scan in a 180 degree arc with his own set of binoculars.

The two police officers could see across the rooftops of the entire town from the old churches bell tower.

"According to Marcus, he got six shots at that thing point blank and the thing did not scratch. You think that thing is going to be any better from two hundred meters?" Officer Reinhold asked as he motioned to Deputy Weiss's .308 rifle and its powerful scope.

"In my hand….. maybe" Geoffrey Weiss responded coolly.

He had spent eight years in the military, and had advanced to third level sniper.

"If there's a weak spot bigger than a bottle cap… definitely." He continued.

"Well one thing's for sure, no matter what we all do to get this thing, Marcus is going to claim the credit." Reinhold moaned.

"Yup"

"Too much politician not enough cop in my opinion."

"Yup"

The radio perched on the half wall of the bell tower crackled, before a voice emanated from it.

"This is George; we're just finishing the sweep down here on Main Street. How are things up there? Over"

Geoffrey picked up the radio and responded.

"We haven't seen a thing in two hours. Over"

"We haven't seen Marcus in a while and he's not picking up his radio. So I guess you're the ranking officer Geoff. You got any instructions from here on? Over" George added.

"You all just stay on the radio, and fan out through town. Stay alert. Over" he instructed.

"Gottcha" crackled back before the radio went silent.

"Marcus! Where is that prick?" Reinhold complained.

"Dunno"

Officer Reinhold appeared disturbed by Deputy Weiss's curt responses.

"How can you not hate that bastard for sandbagging you in the election? You know it was him who started that rumor about you having an illegitimate child?" Reinhold pressed.

Deputy Weiss had left Mornel at eighteen to join the military he returned eight years later with a new bride and an adopted child. The feudal traditions of the small town frowned upon 'outsiders' staking claims in Mornel through marriage. The elders preferred, and tradition dictated, that Mornel residents married 'one of their own'.

Deputy Weiss's bride and their adopted daughter now had the right to own land in the tiny town. It did not help that his daughter was 'colored'. When Geoffrey found the gumption to run against Marcus in the last election, a rumor circulated that Weiss's daughter was his own blood but born to a 'colored' mistress.

"I'm sure that rumor was his." Geoffrey Weiss continued his cool responses.

Officer Reinhold continued to be perplexed by deputy Weiss's lack of venom for Marcus. He thought silently for a long minute about how it could be.

"For the record Geoff, all the boys were pulling for you. You've actually earned the right to run. That prick just rides his name." officer Reinhold continued as he raised his binoculars and again scanned the rooftops of the other 180 degrees surrounding them.

Geoffrey offered no response, as Reinhold continued to ponder Weiss's stoic reaction.

"You know that he's dirty right? I mean he has not gotten caught yet, but you know he's dirty?" Reinhold stated from behind his binoculars.

"Yup" Weiss responded in the now familiar cool tone, still scanning the rooftops on his side of the tower.

"This is what I don't understand; you'll agree that he's dirty, but you tell everyone you're not interested in politics anymore, and you know you're only one who could beat him...... Wait.... You're going to run again aren't you? You're just play'n possum.."

A thin smile briefly flashed beneath Deputy Weiss's binoculars.

A tiny cluster of cells came into focus, as Heisten gently twisted the microscopes fine adjustment knob. A glob of four white cells floating on a light green substrate filled the field.

He lifted his head from the scope and stared silently at a random spot on the wall. He had discovered something and it was apparent from his expression that he was still trying to wrap his mind around it.

After several awkward moments of watching Bernard stare at the wall, Zahra grew impatient.

"Doctor?" she interrupted motioning to the microscope.

"Oh please" Bernard stammered, suddenly remembering his guest, and moving from the front of the microscope.

Zahra leaned into the scope, as Bernard returned his attention to the device. The image resembling the virgin mother still hung over the device. Bernard squatted down to inspect the large disks that had been exposed when the sphere shaped section of it had opened. Each disk was a hive of tiny embedded containers joined together by a network of finely etched groves. The outer edges of the disks where rimmed with a translucent tube. The tube was partitioned internally every four centimeters into tiny compartments that held liquids in various hues of blue and purple.

Across the room, Zahra relinquished the microscope.

Bernard stoked his goatee as he bobbed and weaved his head, peering into the jumble of components. After he had gotten a good look, his motion stopped and he appeared to again be entrenched in some deep thought.

"So.. I don't get it.. What did I just look at?" Zahra asked.

"It's a zygote" Bernard stated confidently.

"Alright... what is that and what does it have to do with the virgin mother?" Zahra followed.

"Well this thing is a gene splicer... Wait.. Wait.. that's not where I should start. Alright, give me one minute to figure out the best way to explain this..." Bernard paced for second before he moved again to his white board.

"So, I will start with some round numbers to make it easy. Let's say one in one hundred stars, which as you know are solar systems just like ours, let's say one in one hundred stars have planets orbiting them. Scientist here call them extrasolar planets because they are not in our system... Then, let's say of those extrasolar planets one in one hundred are in the right orbit.. and I mean

214

by that; not so close to their sun that they are too hot and not so far that they are frozen solid."

"Wait a sec … there are animals that live in the desert, and the arctic." Zahra interjected.

"That's right but all deserts get some rain and evolution suggests that current day deserts were not always such, the organisms that live there slowly adapted to the harsher environment. In other words if the entire planet were desert or ice covered, the simple life forms never would have gotten a foothold enough to spawn the more complex organisms. It is from the wet and temperate climates that life springs. Let me think of an example using something you're familiar with….. OK.. pour salt and sugar on the table and they are not going to react with one another. They are in a solid state. They'll just sit there, the salt grains will always be salt, and the sugar will be sugar. You could sit there forever and nothing will happen. But if they were both dissolved in water… Water moves. The sugar and salt would be floating around in the water colliding with one another. In a fluid environment, a reaction is much more likely to occur." Dr Heisten explained.

"OK , so back to the math… As I said one in a hundred 'stars with planets' , and one in a hundred 'planets in proper orbit' and finally; even if the orbit is right the matter that makes up the planet needs to be diverse. The right temperature is only going to help if you have a diversity of compounds to mix. If the planet is made up entirely of … iron let's say, life is still not going to form. So, we will say another one in one hundred planets will have sufficient variety. If you multiply those odds you end up with one in one million. That is one in one million stars will have a planet similar to ours. Again, these are not the real odds. Do you understand so far?"

Zahra nodded a yes.

"OK now let's say there are only a five hundred stars within a hundred light years from us. Within five hundred light years there are.. ten thousand stars, and within a thousand light years there are a million stars. ….. Based on the odds you have a slim chance of finding that life supporting planet close to you and much better chance the further you can travel. In fact, the overwhelming odds are that a planet like ours will be more than five hundred light years from us." Bernard explained.

"I'm still trying to fit the virgin mother into this." Zahra sighed.

"Please be patient I am just providing the foundation…. Now, the scientific community has been talking about how we would get to extrasolar planets. Giant generation ships that can grow their own food and sustain a colony of space travelers, as they made the voyage to a distant star. The problem is the more mass you try to move the more energy it takes. So, to send a giant ship, and accelerate it to near light

216

speed, would take astronomical amounts of energy. The amount of energy you need multiplies exponentially with each kilo you add to the ship. Now think about what we are doing with the genome mapping project and nanomachines and genetic engineering. What if you could build a compact gene splicer, use the most advanced science we have like nanomachines, and take something's genetic code and make a tiny step more human? One tiny mutation at a time over thousands of years.. In other words you build this compact device and you send it off to a planet you know is capable of sustaining life. There will likely already be the beginnings of life on the planet, because there is another simple rule; if it can occur, over along enough timeline, it will have occurred. But as a precaution you carry just a simple single celled organism to start with. ... "

"Is that what we were looking at in the microscope?" Zahra queried

"Hold on, I'm getting to that... perhaps we should play the animation again." Heisten answered, as he motioned for Zahra to turn off the light switch and again tapped the downward triangle to reverse the holographic presentation. Once the animation had returned to the beginning, Heisten restarted it.

They stood silently watching the animation of the pill like container moving through space. It was not until the device ejected from the pill and splashed down in the ocean that Heisten again began to speak.

"You see when it landed it went to the shore line to see if intelligent life had advanced yet from the ocean.... It had not, only vegetation and simple organisms had moved to the land... I am guessing this is around the Devonian period.. maybe two hundred million years ago. That first animal the animation shows is the lungfish.. Evolutionary science has long hypothesized this fish was the first to come onto the land. This was based on the design of those weird arm like fins. It's believed this fin mutation happened and it allowed the lungfish to lay its eggs at the waters edge where the fish's normal predators could not reach them. This was an advantage..... Now, the lungfish was the most advanced organism it could find. So it scans it, samples an egg from the fish, and edits the eggs genetic code, to make it more reptilian.... And one step closer to us.

Then it drops the fertilized egg at the waters edge.... Maybe it finds a few more and does the same thing just to be sure the next genetic step is going to be taken... then it hibernates for a hundred, or even a thousand years..."

"How does this thing run this long?" Zahra again interjected.

"I don't know yet.. I mean this is light years ahead of us... We're still running internal combustion engines. This thing seems to run entirely on whatever ambient

218

energy is available. ...   Now, when this thing wakes up it again seeks out the most advanced life form, now it finds lizards.   It does the same thing sampling an egg and dropping in some more code. "

Heisten began to speed up the animation again.

"And you can see the device edged the lizards toward rodent like animals, then slowly primate like animals like the lemur, then monkeys,   then more advanced primates, then the stages of prehistoric man start to unfold.   The device inserting key mutations into the mix every few hundred years."

As the modern humans began to emerge from the images, Bernard once again froze the animation.

"Now, think for a moment about the course of recorded human history..... Just since we started writing things down...   Every major era fueled by a handful of men.   You had a spiritual revolution fueled by a great prophet and another man millions believed to be the son of god.   An age of philosophy an age of conquest and discovery, a renaissance age and the age of reason.   All of these periods of great advancement fueled by a handful of men; of similar age, from the same general geographic area.   The great philosophers, were all from the same area and time. The great renaissance artists and inventors, they were from the same region and time.   The great composers, even the great scientists and engineers of the industrial age all born near here at about the same time. .. So my theory is this: I think the mothers of some of the greatest men in human history are displayed here in this hologram. " Heisten finished his explanation as he started the animation.

They carefully examined the images of modern human women as they passed by.

Heisten's hypothesis seemed to make sense. The women did seem familiar, and they appeared to be dressed in clothes representative of the ages Bernard had listed. Zahra gasped as she realized the final holographic image was her own.

"The zygote on that microscope stage is yours Zahra. It's from one of your eggs." Bernard concluded in an unsurprised and gentle tone.

"I'm ready to go" Laura's voice crackled from the intercom.

Father Joilen had returned just in time to escort Laura and Heidi to their temporary accomodations. He opened the door of the old feed house cautiously. He and Laura had not noticed the muddy ATV tracks as they approached the front of the tiny cabin. Jolien scanned the dark cabin with the flashlight he had been issued by Bernard. Soon Laura, with an exhausted Heidi cradled in her arms, was in the doorway beside him.   Laura brought her own flash light to bare on the dark void of the cabins interior.   It was empty as far as they could tell, and everything appeared to be in the same condition Jolien had remembered.

Hesitant to turn on the eletric lighting for fear or waking Heidi; the old priest retrieved pack of matches from the kitchen counter and lit an oil lamp.   The lamp light illuminated the cabin enough to navigate without the aid of flashlights, but not so much to wake a sleeping child.

He then turned his attention to the wood stove, loading it up with two logs and load of kindling, and paper.   The room was soon brightened further by the wedges of light that slipped through the thick tempered glass of the woodstove's door.   Jolien retrieved the comforters from the loft and draped them over chairs near the stove. Laura started the tea kettle and electric oven to expedite the heating of the cabin, as she continued to hold her sleeping child.

He was anxious to return to the Heisten compound and look after Zahra, but he had promised Bernard that he would make sure Laura and Heidi were safe and comfortable before he returned.   Laura's fear of the device had turned into near contempt for the people who had brought it into her world.   He sensed the uneasy tension from Laura, and he understood her perspective; she was enjoying a holiday with her father, and now she found herself holed up in a rustic cabin, with an old priest she hardly knew. It did not help that the sleeping Heidi prevented conversation above a whisper. The two sat silently watching the flickering fire through the thick discolored glass of the wood stove. Jolien quickly jumped up to turn off the hissing tea pot before it developed into its screeching whistle. A peace offering of herbal tea might help kill some time, and settle their equally frayed nerves. He quietly concocted the beverages in the dim light of the chalet as Laura sat entranced by the flickering fire.

He expected to stay another two hours, until the cabin had warmed and Laura and Heidi were both asleep. He would then return to the rectory to spend the morning collecting any news of other sightings or additional cassualties, and attending to his flock.

Laura smiled as she shifted Heidi in her arms and positioned herself to accept the mug she was being offered. A smile that signaled a warming of tensions, and gave Father Jolien hope that the next two hours would not seem as long as he first expected. Jolien waited for the cabin to heat watching Laura silently rocking Heidi in her arms, and thinking about his own daughter.

Under the vaulted ceiling of Bernard Heisten's great room, Zahra sat on the floor in front of a fireplace large enough to roast a pig. The fire was sizable, but appeared small framed by such a large hearth. Zahra stared intently and unflinching at the burning logs. The tapping of Bernard's shoes against the hardwood floors provoked no response from Zahra, and she appeared startled as Bernard addressed her.

"Are you alright?"

"Yeah.... Yeah I think so." Zahra exhaled. Heisten surveyed her for moment before parking himself in a leather chair that faced her.

"This old man is tired... I am sure you are not tired... There must be a thousand things running through your mind now, and I know you only woke up a few hours ago.

"Bernard waited for a response, but Zahra sat entranced by the fire and her own thoughts.

"Zahra." Bernard leaned toward her and lowered his voice an octave to gain her attention. Zahra turned from the fire and looked up at Dr Heisten,

"I know you've got a lot on your mind. It's got to be disturbing that something from another world has grabbed a piece of your body. Especially something like an egg, but I have to tell you again how confident I am that this thing is not out to hurt us."

"It's tough to have everything you've ever believe about God and who we are crushed like this. Everything you've been taught for years." Zahra released with a labored sigh

"Zahra it may surprise you to know that I consider myself a very spiritual person… I think it is a mistake to see this as an affront to God. Religious texts have been written and rewritten over the ages usually to suit political needs. If you take real lessons from the text and leave out all the nonsense about who begot who, and all the rules that you know just don't make any sense in your heart; you'll see, Zahra, that the device is a gift from God. I don't know if we'll ever find the origin of this device. But, if it was designed to foster rudimentary life forms into us, than surely our spirit is in that design somewhere."

Heisten pleaded, as Zahra listened intently.

"I believe the people that made this device found the code the essence of spirituality that drives us to look for answers to our past and our future. I believe that desire; to know the past, to know our origin, and to seek truth, is the foundation for all spirituality. All these organized religions; they are all seekers, albeit under different flags." Bernard continued his impassioned plea.

"Why did it have to choose me?" Zahra protested.

"We don't always choose our path Zahra. I wish it were easier…. I can tell you what I believe though:

I believe we are a species that can ask the question 'Who are we?'; Whether you believe

224

that there is a divine creator of all that we are, and all that we have, or whether you believe that we are the result of a long sequence of chance mutations that sculpted us into who we are; you have to recognize that the ability to ask that question makes us very special. Special enough that our story should continue. Continue past the life span of this single star. I believe it's our DUTY to explore new solar systems new galaxies. It's our DUTY to survive, and that is why I feel connected to this device. This device is about survival, and exploration.... While you were up here, I reran the animation one more time, and I browsed the other section of the holograph menu. It had detailed plans for both the device and two other ships to transport it though space."

He paused for a moment, as he slid off his chair and onto the floor next to her. He took her hand in his, as he continued to make his case for trusting the device.

"Zahra, please listen to my theory because I think I've come to some other conclusions about the device." Heisten implored.

Zahra's brow twinged at the assertion she was about to be given another revelation to digest.

"Now, please just be patient and listen as I explain these two things..." Bernard prefaced as he searched for a place to begin.

"In middle school, during a discussion of the big bang, I asked my teacher 'Why does there have to be a beginning?'

225

My teacher replied snidely; 'Everything has a beginning. Name me one thing that has no beginning.'

Now, I knew my question had merit but I was not yet armed with the knowledge of tropic levels and life cycles and the principle that matter can neither be created nor destroyed. I did not mean to say that the universe did not explode out from a single point. My point was that the singular point could have held all the mass of the universe. A mass so compact under its own gravitation force that it could fit in the palm of a hand. "

Bernard illustrated the compacted universe by holding up his clenched fist.

"But the heaviest atoms are the most unstable. Uranium for example. Maybe the Universe, packed so densely, would be so unstable that the slightest impact from a tiny mass would cause an explosion.. And BOOM out spins the universe. So extrapolating the scenario further; it is possible that the energy release from the bang accelerates the universe outward. Now during the expansion; stars are forming and masses are clumping together to form planets as the debris of this explosion moves outward. As the explosion's energy dissipates, the acceleration slows. The matter of the universe eventually reaches cruising speed. But here is the thing: If mass attracts mass, then the matter at the distant edges of the universe would all have more matter behind them than in front, as they moved outward. The slight gravitational pull of the universe behind these remote stars would start to slow their outward thrust. Until eons later they would stop, and then begin their journey back inward to the center of the universe. As mass once again gathered in the center of the universe, the gravitational pull toward the center would become stronger. The universe would once again collapse to the size of a fist. And maybe one tiny particle that shot out from the bang and traveled the furthest outward would finally come to stop. Maybe, after all the matter had collected at the center, this tiny particle would finally begin its journey back to the center. This holdout that had enough energy to resist the pull, would then begin its rapid convergence on the now unstable mass of the universe. Like an electron fired at the center of a giant unstable atom. And once again, BANG!

Maybe this is how it goes... forever. A finite universe, collapsing and expanding, pulsing along on an infinite timeline."

Zahra pondered the concept for a moment. She measured his answer for the eschatological question against her own thoughts. The entire conversation made surreal by the dancing shadows of the flickering firelight.

"That's depressing... I mean what good is all this? Why worry about exploring the universe if in the end everything is going to be sucked back into a lifeless mass?" Zahra challenged.

"What if it were possible to send a small device to the edge of the universe. Propel it even further out as the next implosion begins. Then, as the gravitational pull to the center becomes too great, thrust in lateral direction to the pull. If the acceleration to the center can be pulled off to the side with sufficient force perhaps the center can be avoided, and the device can sling shot past all the matter in the universe and enter an immense elliptical orbit. Like a tiny electron whipping around the compressed universe. Perhaps that orbit can be maintained until the next big bang."

Zahra continued to stare into the flickering fire as she pondered Dr Heisten's assertion.

"If we could make such a device what would we put in it? The sum of our scientific knowledge, philosophical writings, great works of art, scripture, Music? I had the thought that somewhere in that vessel down stairs there was a chip with all those things stored inside, and I believe I found it." Bernard stated.

From his breast pocket he produced a coin sized octagonal crystal mounted to the center of what appeared to be a printed circuit. He offered it to Zahra. And she took it in her hand, holding it up to let the crystal catch the firelight.

"I think that vessel is here to give us the head start we need to survive." entreated Bernard.

Zahra seemed less distant the more Bernard gave her to think about.

"What do you think is on it?" Zahra asked.

"We'll start working on that question in the morning."

"If what you're saying is true, Dr Heisten, then that thing might be the most important item in the universe." Zahra noted.

"I think that would be a valid assumption… And here's the second thing. "
Zahra took a breath and braced herself for another revelation.

"I also have more insight into how the gene splicing functions work. The device tagged you with that transmitter because it needed time to analyze your DNA and develop mutations your body would not reject. It finished that analysis then fertilized your egg, as it spliced in its changes. The egg then split into two cells. Once fertilized, I'm sure the device would have wasted no time in tracking you down via that transmitter, so that it could reinsert the cells. When we found the zygote it was four cells. The zygote has split into eight cells now, by morning it will be sixteen. It will keep doubling every twelve hours. By tomorrow afternoon, I am not sure that the machine will be able to reinsert the zygote. It will be too large." Heisten warned.

"Re-insert? You want to let this thing impregnate me?" Zahra protested.

"Zahra, I can't tell you what to do, but if you had considered it; I thought you should know your window of opportunity is closing." Heisten explained.

"I had not considered it." Zahra shot Bernard a doubious glare.

"I'm sorry. I don't want it to appear like I'm trying to get you to do something you don't want to. However, I have to tell you that I believe this might be an opportunity for the human race that we may never get back." Bernard pleaded.

"Dr. Heisten this is not asking me to give up a weekend to help at ahh.. soup kitchen or something. This is my entire life. Having a baby, raising it, you're asking me to give up my life!"

"You're right. It is a huge sacrifice, but I am telling you this child will be special... and let me clarify something: I am not suggesting you decide whether to keep the child. It can be aborted later if you decide you can't do it. But we have to get the zygote off that slide and into your body if we want to have any options at all." Bernard persisted.

"You say that like aborting a fetus is nothing! Oh God why is this happening to me?! " Zahra moaned as tears formed in her eyes. Dr. Heisten realized he was being far too clinical in his discussion.

"Can't someone else take it?" Zahra sobbed.

"Zahra, how are we going to find a girl similar enough to you genetically to accept your baby, AND convince her to have a baby, in the next twelve hours?" Bernard asked gently.

Zahra buried her face in her hands as she sniffed and choked down the tears that were welling in her sinuses.

"Perhaps I should have waited for Father Jolien to come back before discussing this with you. Admittedly these types of ethical questions are not my forte." Bernard added with a note of regret, as he waited for Zahra to regain her composure.

"What do you think she would be like?" Zahra finally asked.

"She?"

"The baby…. I always picture myself having a little girl." Zahra clarified.

"Oh, it will be a boy most assuredly, more efficient for spreading an upgrade to the gene pool.. I imagine he'll have a pretty strong libido." Heisten surmised.

"Great!.. I get to bear a little alien horn dog." Zahra chuckled

"No, Not alien, there would be no 'us' if not for whoever built this thing, We already are a primitive version of whatever they are." Heisten reminded Zahra.

"The thing is, Zahra, that this child will be brilliant at something. I don't know what he'll be brilliant at, but it may be something we desperately need. You'll be one of the great mothers of history… Those women that the device displayed were the mothers of the great renaissance artists, the great philosophers, the great spiritual leaders, the great composers, the great mathematicians and physicists...."

"I just can't do it, and I could never abort a baby." Zahra exhaled.

"Well, if you believe life begins at fertilization, then there is a life on that dish in the lab that will die unless you accept it."

"That makes me feel great!" Zahra protested.

"Again, I'm sure Father Jolien's council on this matter will be more helpful. I will leave you alone now, perhaps talk it over with him when he comes back. I hope he'll be here before morning. The sun will be up in few hours. I removed the transmitter from Milo. It's clean and sitting on a petri dish in the lab. First thing in the morning we'll need to make a decision.... Whether or not to reinsert it and turn the device back on....."

Dr. Heisten hesitated for a moment, before kissing Zahra on the forehead as he got up to take his leave. It was an awkward display of sympathy, from the Dr. rapidly trying to develop a bedside manor.

"Goodnight Dr. Heisten" Zahra sighed.

"Goodnight.." Bernard smiled as he turned to leave. "Oh there is one last item, and maybe this will make the difference for you... The last girl on the animation before your image... I recognized her. When I grew up here, some seventy years ago now, there was a woman, a handmaid. She had a son a year older than me. She stuck in my memory as she was the only single mother in the town. She died in a hiking accident when I was about seven years old. Father Jolien's mother was the last to be impregnated by the device. He's a very special man, compassionate, understanding, forgiving, but if he is a fruit of this device he has not passed it on. He has not had children."

Zahra flashed a puzzled look at Bernard.

"Father Jolien???"

"Nurture won out over nature. Social pressures stopped him from passing on his genes." Heisten explained.

"What does that have to do with me?" Zahra questioned.

"I don't know how many times the device injects the same genetic code into the pool. So, if he did not pass it on it could be lost. Or it could be that your zygote is the only one left with that code. I just can't say for sure if something was lost or not." Heisten concluded. An odd silence followed the revelation. The Dr. again struggled to find a comforting act he could provide the troubled young girl before him.

"Shall I get a bed ready for you upstairs, do you need anything?" he asked.

"… No I'll be ok. Thank you, but I'll try to sleep down here and wait for Father Jolien." Zahra finaly answered.

Sheriff Brein peered through the thick wall of pine trees just down hill from Zahra chalet. In the half light of the early morning, he could just make out smoke now billowing from the roof's stove pipe. He checked his watch as Father Jolien emerged from the chalet and began his trek down the trail that would take him back to town. Marcus had just been 'informed' by deputy Wiess that Father Jolien had a daughter. The priest's sudden candor about his illegitimate child left Marcus with little leverage over the old priest. Marcus was also leery of the timing of his confession. The old priest had been somehow sparked to candor by the death of Adeline. Perhaps he would need to be dealt with, but right now Marcus was focused on the device, and Zahra. The smoke that continued billowing from the stove pipe suggested she had returned. He dismounted his ATV as the old priest disappeared down the trail, and stealthily approached the chalet.

Through the dirty glass windows of the old feed house he could see Laura Heisten, as she slept cradling Heidi in her arms. He recognized her.

Quietly, he crept to the front window, where he would have a better view of the loft.

On his way he passed the muddy footprints of Laura and Father Jolien. Just two sets he noted.

From the front porch again he scanned the room through a dirty glass window.
She was alone.

Father Jolien had planned a quick stop at his chambers to shower and change before checking in with Sister Gershan, who answered the rectory phone and generally managed the church affairs. As soon as was possible, he would be heading back up to Heisten's villa. No sooner had he turned off the shower, when the harsh electric repine of his door buzzer startled him. The sun had just risen and the chamber was brightening with natural light. He tightened his robe and shook his head as he made his way to the front door of his humble domicile. He opened his door to find Sister Gershan. She was an elderly woman whose habit and horn rimmed glasses made her look cartoonish.

"I'm sorry father but you did not answer your phone." Sister Gershan explained.

"That's alright, what seems to be the problem." A groggy Father Jolien muttered.

"Well Deputy Wiess phoned, and said he required your services for another poor lad they found on the mountain last night."

"OK, thanks, I'll contact him as soon as I'm dressed." Jolien replied as he motioned to close the door.

"No he said…. "Sister Gershan referred to a note pad. "you should head on up the

Riffleberg trail until you reach the reservoir then head west until you hit the top of the gorge. Said he'll be waiting up there."

"So deputy Weiss said it was urgent?" Jolien wondered.

"I didn't note that, but calling this early, I imagine it is."

Father Jolien usually only got emergency calls when a man was still alive but near death. The spot Sister Gershan had noted was about two kilometers up the mountain from Heisten compound. He thought for a second about who would likely be at that location of the mountain.

XII : Music

Dr. Heisten could not remember the last time he had felt so awake after getting so little sleep. He was excited to get to work, and his brain had woken him at the first opportunity.

He descended the stairs noting how quiet the house seemed. He had become accustomed to Laura and Heidi's playful banter emanating from the kitchen when he awoke. Reaching the bottom of the stair, he passed the couch, where Zahra slept. He could not see her from behind the couch but moved quietly as not to disturb her.

The florescent bulbs of the kitchens overhead lights sputtered to life automatically as he entered the room. Heisten lifted a tea kettle from the range, measuring its weight before taking it to the sink. Heisten filled the kettle in anticipation of Zahra awakening and placed it on the stove. The door to the Heisten's basement lab fed into the kitchen. Bernard glanced at the door for a moment before deciding he should get to work.

The long basement stairs were illuminated by a single bulb at the top. Bernard descended into the darkened lab and fumbled for a moment for the switch. Randomly, the chain of florescent bulbs that dotted the ceiling 'tinked' and flickered until the entire lab was saturated in cool white light.

Heisten was shocked to turn and find Zahra staring him in the face with a swatch of duct tape covering her mouth. She had been bounded around the wrists using disposable 'zip tie' handcuffs. Between her arms ran the black iron gas line that fed the house from the propane tank outside the house. Bernard was frozen, unable to react.

"Good morning Dr." Crept into Bernard's ear from behind. The greeting was followed clack of a pistol cocking.

Bernard turned to find Marcus Brein's pistol trained at his torso.

"Is there a problem here?" Bernard asked unsure of Brein's intentions.

"Yeah, there is a big problem this thing killed my grandfather and young girl!" he lied. "..and now it has to go." Marcus finished callously.

Bernard noticed the device had been closed and now levitated once more in the center of the room.

"I assure you officer that this device did not intentionally kill anyone." Heisten pleaded.

"This is not up for debate. You can help me destroy this thing or you can die." Marcus shouted, as he raised his gun to Bernard's head.

"Wait, let me explain… we figured it out.." Heisten pleaded.

"What's inside?" Marcus interrupted.

Bernard quickly assessed the situation. He calculated that Zahra had closed the device in an attempt to protect it. This was a good move; since the shell of this device had protected it from the pressure and temperature extremes of both entering the atmosphere, and of being packed in the glacier. The device seemed indestructible when closed.

"I don't know that it does open." Bernard lied.

Marcus took a step toward Dr Heisten.

"Zahra over there already tried to convince me to bow to that unholy thing. She told me all about tubes and wires and holograms... So you wanna change that story?" Marcus sneered.

"It opened for a while but we are unsure how it happened.." Bernard again lied.

Marcus' face again winced in anger.

"Alright, old man this is your last chance you've got ten seconds to start opening that thing.... And no more bullshit! Zahra already spilled the beans about how some chemicals open the device, but she did not know the sequence... ten.. nine... eight" Marcus began his count down.

"Wait let's calm down here"

"seven.... six"

"This thing might be the key to preserving mankind." Bernard pleaded.

"five.. four" Marcus continued in an icy tone.

"If you destroy this, you destroy your creator."

"Don't you dare blaspheme old man! Two" Marcus continued as he raised his aim to Bernard's head.

"OK .." Bernard stated. He would not open the device to this madman, but he needed to buy time. Bernard turned his back to Marcus and faced the table behind the device.

"You got one minute.. and you try anything over there, it's lights out." Marcus demanded as the tea pot upstairs began to whistle.

Bernard retrieved an empty syringe, but instead of reaching for one of the beakers he had prepared the day before, his hand found a brown bottle he knew to contain boric acid. He quickly filled the syringe with the concentrated and deadly acid. While Marcus was focused on Dr. Heisten Zahra continued to try and pull her now bloody hands trough the tough nylon binding. Bernard palmed the syringe with boric acid in one hand and collected a handful of empty syringes in the other before turning to Marcus.

"I'm going to need you to come over here and help.. the chemicals have to be injected simultaneously..." Bernard coaxed.

Marcus leered at Bernard suspiciously, as the kettle upstairs continued to bellow loudly.

"Come on, the Xeon isotopes break down in less than a minute." Bernard again lied. Marcus could not argue science, and the doctor's gibberish seemed like the real thing. Marcus glanced at Zahra and quickly assessed the option of releasing her to assist the old man. The kettles violent whistle, dulled by distance and barriers, seemed much louder to the ears of Zahra and Bernard. Marcus concluded that taking his gun off the old man was less a threat than releasing Zahra. Marcus approached Bernard who had extended his hand offering him the cluster of empty syringes. Bernard's other hand tightened around the acid filled syringe.

Marcus was within in arms length of Bernard and reaching for the empty syringes when his motion was interrupted by the sudden stop of the steam whistle. Marcus was now aware of someone else in the house. He turned to glance up the stairs and Bernard saw an opportunity to pounce. Bernard grasped the acid filled syringe like a dagger and lunged at Marcus driving the syringe deep into his neck. Marcus tilted his pistol upward and squeezed off a round just as the needle broke the surface. Dr Heisten's neck snapped as the back of his skull exploded in a cloud of red. The blood spatter fanned across the back wall of the lab, and blow back sprayed across the front of Marcus.

"FATHER!" Laura yelled from the kitchen as the gun shot echoed through the house.

" are you alright?" Laura called sheepishly from the top of the stairs, unaware the loud but muffled bang she heard through the basement door was a gunshot.

242

Marcus gently removed the syringe from his neck, contorting his face. The plunger had not been depressed. Zahra continued her fight with the nylon handcuffs, as Laura's footsteps echoed from the stairwell.

Laura spotted her father first and ran to his side nearly tripping on the final step of the basement stairs. Dr Heisten lay on his side as pool of blood developed underneath the levitating device.

"Dad?!" Laura exclaimed. Lifting his bloody disfigured head into her lap as an angry Marcus Brein approached her from behind unrolling a swatch of duct tape as he moved.

Marcus gagged and bound Laura with brutal efficiency, as she rolled frantically on the blood soaked basement floor.

"Momma?" came softly down the basement stairs as everyone froze.

Marcus Brein grimaced again before mouthing a silent expletive.

"I'm gonna take this tape off, and if you care about you daughter you'll tell her to run, tell her there is a fire and she needs to run to town and get help…. Do you understand? You tell her that before she takes one step down those stairs." Marcus whispered in Laura's ear as he pressed his knee into her back.

243

He allowed Laura a moment to process his request before ripping the duct tape from her mouth.

"Honey!" Laura yelled in a stuffy but calm tone.

"Don't come down here. There's a fire... I need you to run to town just as fast as you can, alright?!" Laura continued fight back tears.

"I want you to come momma." Heidi pleaded as she took one step down the creaky stairs.

"Baby don't come down here!" Laura yelled sternly now.

"You need to run outside and head down the trail to town. I need you to be a big girl now, and help momma." Laura yelled.

"But Momma..." An upset Heidi began to cry as Marcus lifted Laura to her feet.

"Please Heidi, run to town for momma. Be a big girl!!" Laura screamed.

Heidi paused for moment at the top the stairs, before turning and running out of the kitchen and into the backyard. Tears were beginning to run down Heidi's face as she crossed the courtyard and exited the gates.

Marcus removed the duct tape from Zahra's mouth. She could only turn to Marcus with a hate in her eyes.

"What the hell is wrong with you!" She shouted.

The blood spattered Marcus turned his gun on Zahra.

"Shut Up! .. unless you want to be next!"
Marcus fired back.

Marcus's was trying to figure out his next move. Things were spiraling out of control on Marcus. The girl, the priest, the doctor if necessary; these were the only ones he had thought about sacrificing.

"Hey, just let her go." Zahra begged as she motioned with her eyes to the distraught Laura as she leaned against the wall weeping.

"I am going to ask you one more time; Do you know how to open this thing?" Marcus gritted his teeth as he wiped the spattered blood from his face.

"I told you I'm not sure of the sequence." Zahra sputtered.

Marcus took a step toward Zahra raising his gun to her head.

"Well here's the deal; if you can't open it you're no longer any use to me so I'm gonna give you one chance to open it.... Then I'm gonna kill you... So can you open it or not?" Marcus said spitting through his clenched teeth.

"Yeah, I think so.." a shaking Zahra confessed.

Marcus removed a small knife from his holster. He hastily severed the nylon cuffs nicking Zahra's already bloody hands.

"You better hope that you can little girl. You've got one minute, and if that thing is not open, you're dead." Marcus threatened.

Zahra could not find the will to move with the gun trained on her. Marcus lowered his weapon and stepped to the side to allow her access to the lab table.

"Move!" He prodded her.

Zahra, still shaking, approached the table and began sorting through the beakers and lab paraphernalia that were splayed across it. Her hands shook as she fumbled to grasp each item. Occasionally she would use her wrists to clear the tears that were welling in her eyes. She shuttered as she nearly lost her footing in what she knew was the pool of Bernard's blood. The ever-present weeping of Laura Heisten did nothing to lessen Zahra's anxiety. Marcus was unrelenting with his prodding of the shaken girl : "thirty seconds!"

Zahra quickly prepared the syringes again drawing what little of the solutions remained in the beakers. Zahra fought to maintain her composer, as she had to look down at Dr Heisten's corpse to avoid tripping over it. Bernard's cleanly shaven bald head did nothing to hide the gruesome wound from which blood and grey mater oozed. Soon, Zahra's shaking hands were finding the appropriate holes for each syringe in the back of the device. She injected each in turn hoping she had gotten the placement of each correct.

"Five seconds!"

Zahra finished her task, and stood silently praying for the device open.

After a tense moment, the device dropped to the ground and opened again with a hiss.

Marcus's eyes widened as the machines innards were revealed.

"Get back over there.." Marcus mumbled still surveying the machine.

Zahra again shuttered in disgust at the sound of tacky squishing noise that was Bernard's blood under her feet.

Marcus circled the device before waving his hand through the Hologram, as if he expected to feel the symbols. His hand glanced at the double helix first and the animation that was now familiar to Zahra again began to play. Marcus stood silently and watched. As the animation reached the part where genes were being spliced Zahra chimed in:

"It's showing you what it does... It found some basic life forms and advanced them."

Marcus bore a strange grimace as he watched the animation.

"If you hit the upward pointing triangle it will fast forward, and then you'll see." Zahra suggested.

Marcus fast forwarded the animation.

"Do you see the mammals just became early primates?" Zahra narrated.

Marcus seemed more and more angry as the animation progressed.

"This is blasphemy!" Marcus screamed.

Zahra suddenly realized she would not be able to reach Marcus with reason, and remembered that her image was on the last frame of the animation.

"You can stop it just by hitting the downward triangle a few times" Zahra offered.

Marcus stopped the animation at the image of Father Jolien's mother.

"This is the devils trick! How could you all be so stupid!" Marcus yelled.

Zahra was happy the agitated psychotic in front of her had not reached her image.

"It's just like all those fossils. Put here to trick us... don't you understand that!?" Marcus ranted.

Zahra clung to the still weeping Laura as she tried to get some reading on how to defuse the situation.

"The universe AND MAN were created by the lord no more than five thousand years ago! Don't you understand this is just a test of faith?" Marcus screamed at his two scared hostages. Their faces portrayed terror and disbelief, which only further angered Marcus. He approached Zahra and placed the barrel of his gun against her temple, as he grabbed her by the hair.

"NO NO NO" pleaded Zahra.

"I want to hear you say that you believe in god!" Marcus demanded as he cocked his gun once more. Zahra shuttered at the clank of the hammer next to her ear.

"OK OK, I believe in god... OK" Zahra stammered

"And who created the universe!?" Marcus demanded.

"God" Zahra answered.

"Let me hear you too!" Marcus directed Laura as he tugged Zahra's hair

"G-ggod" Laura sputtered.

Marcus removed the baton from his belt, as he threw Zahra to the ground behind him. Her prosthetic twisted and cracked as she spun awkwardly to the floor.

He then leaned into Laura until their noses almost touched.

"You heathens need to be reeducated on the ways of the lord. You've lost your way, and the lord requires penitence. You know what that means?" Marcus spewed into Laura's face, as she gave no response.

"That means you get on your knees!" Marcus hollered as he brought his baton down across the side of Laura's leg. Marcus drove the baton with his full force, and Laura's knee popped inward ripping the inside ligaments free.

Laura screamed in pain and dropped to the ground again.

"You little bitches need to be hobbled." Marcus spewed as he lifted her remaining good leg and again smashed his baton down on her knee cap with his full force.

Laura again screamed and dragged herself away from Marcus and into the corner of the lab.

With Laura now hobbled and cowering in the corner, Marcus turned his attention to Zahra, whose prosthetic limb was now clearly visible.

"I almost forgot you were the little bitch who lost her leg here a few years ago…. Looks like half the job was done for me." Marcus smiled.

"You don't have to do this" Zahra pleaded as she tried to crawl away from Marcus.

"I think you might be cursed!" Marcus laughed as he grabbed her prosthetic and yanked it off along with her sweat pants.

"Stop it!" Zahra exclaimed as Marcus grabbed the foot of her good leg.

The baton again fell hard against the side of Zahra's knee, as the sound of cracking bone and tearing ligaments filled the room.

Zahra clutched at her good leg pitching her torso toward Marcus. He quickly holstered his baton and grabbed her by the hair dragging her over to the corner where Laura cowered. Again, the brutal lessons of faith his father had inflicted upon him flashed through his mind; 'Sometimes the lord requires sacrifice' . He could feel his father's leather against his back.

Marcus removed two more zip ties from his jacket pocket.

"I've spent too much time here already. I have an appointment I have to attend to." Marcus commented as he shackled Zahra and Laura to a thick sewer pipe.

"OK. Listen, I'm just a guest in your country.. just take me to the border and let me go. No one is going to believe anything I say." Zahra reasoned.

"That might have been an option until the doctor over there tried to play hero." Marcus sneered as he walked to the corner of the lab were he had left a small duffle bag.

Marcus took the bag over to the lab table and began removing its contents. Inside was a bottle of charcoal lighter fluid, and four bright red cylinders with square boxes attached to the ends. Marcus began spraying the lighter fluid around the lab, applying extra accelerant to the already flammable areas of the lab, and the ceiling joists. He emptied the bottle by sending a trail of accelerant up the stair case and into the kitchen.

"What are you doing?" Zahra pleaded.

Marcus gabbed one of the cylinders from the table and squatted to address Laura and Zahra.

"Well this is a timed charge... The avalanche crews use these in the winter time. I am going to take this one and blow that thing up, and when it blows up this place is going to burn to the ground. and leave no trace of Dr Heisten... or you two heathens." Marcus added with a sinister grin.

"Oh god, he's going to kill us." Laura sobbed.

Marcus stood up and turned a dial on the charge.

"Let's see, it will take the little girl fifteen minutes to get to town. What do you think, twenty minutes enough time for me to be long gone, and back in town with an alibi?" Marcus joked.

Zahra was crying uncontrollably now, her raw and bloodied hands continued to pull against the tough nylon binding.

Marcus stuffed the charge into the jumble of tubes along the back of the device.

He set the timer on another charge and surveyed the room for a place to put it. His eye spotted a ventilation duct in the ceiling. He quickly jammed his fisted into the vent cover, cracking it open. He then tossed the charge a short distance down the duct.

Marcus tossed another charge behind the large chemical closet in the corner of the lab. "I'll set this last one were you can see it, and watch the count down... twenty minutes" Marcus walked to the center of the room and laid the final charge on the floor with the timer facing Laura and Zahra.

"You can't leave us here.... I swear we will never say a word about this if you just get us out of here." Zahra made a final plea as Marcus began moving for the door.

"You should repent in your final minutes; maybe god will have pity on your souls...."

In a bizarre last move Marcus bent down to grab Zahra's prosthetic from the ground before exiting.

"Go to hell!" Zahra screamed as she yanked even harder on her cuffs.

"No, you'll go to hell, because God cares not for accomplishment, only obedience…

...obedience." Marcus stated smugly as he slammed the laboratory door.

Father Jolien approached the rendezvous point that he had been directed to. An officer stood at the top of the gorge with his back facing the trail. Father Jolien paused when the officer turned to face him.

"Glad you could make it Father." Marcus Brein smiled.

Father Jolien surveyed Marcus for a moment.

"Where's deputy Weiss?" Jolien queried.

"He had to go back to town." Marcus lied.

"You've got blood on your jacket." Jolien noted.

"Yeah, it's a bloody mess over there... most people jump from up here. This kid decided to blow his head off."

"A lot of bad things seem to be happening lately."

"Yeah, well he's right behind that rock near the ledge. Have a look."

Marcus pointed to a large boulder that sat just next to the edge of the gorge. From behind the rock a single foot protruded. Marcus had used Zahra's prosthetic to help execute his plan. The old priest at first did not recognize the leg as a fake.

"Marcus. Why did you get me up here? Do you really think I am going to stand on that ledge with you behind me?" the old priest smiled.

Marcus shook his head.

"Well Father I was really hoping not to have to use my throw weapon today. But if you insist." Marcus sneered as he pulled a nine millimeter pistol from his jacket pocket.

"We're running out of time." Laura sobbed, as Zahra mashed her teeth against the tough plastic bindings. The one timer they could see showed four minutes remaining.

"What the fuck is this stuff made from?" She shouted in disgust, glancing again the timer. Zahra paused for moment as Laura continued to weep. She looked down at her left had that was still blistered and burnt, in addition to the latest cuts and bruises.

As if suddenly possessed Zahra sat up and began smashing her left fist against the wall. She punched the wall with all her might, screaming out each time. As her left hand drove into the concrete distinct sounds of bones breaking could be heard. After a dozen impacts Zahra grabbed her mutilated hand and yanked the fingers outward. She let a barbaric scream as the broken bones pulled out from her wrist. With one last yank her mangled and bloody left hand was free. Laura sat shocked by what she had just witnessed.

Zahra crawled on the knees of her twisted legs to the nearest lab table. She reached up and hoisted herself until she stood, with her amputated stub bearing the weight of her body. It was an awkward balancing act made more difficult by the uselessness of her left hand. Frantically, she searched for a something to free Laura. She grabbed the first beaker she spotted and smashed it against the edge of the table. Then, fell back to the floor, retaining a large shard of glass in her good hand. She crawled back to Laura on her forearms, like a solider under barb wire.

Reaching her, she pulled herself up the black iron pipe. The glass dagger she held tightly was already digging into her remain good hand, as she applied the edge of the glass to Laura's zip tie cuffs.

"Lean back, pull your hands tight again the pipe!" Zahra demanded, and Laura complied.

"Hold still." Zahra commanded as she began franticly hacking at the nylon restraint. Both of Zahra's hands were now spouting blood. Laura grimaced as Zahra's slashing stokes caught her wrists and hands in the process, cutting bloody gouges in her delicate skin.

A few more hacks and Laura's cuffs snapped sending her backward toward the door.

"Get out! NOW!" Zahra Screamed.

"I'm not leaving without you!" Laura cried.

255

"There's no time, get out I'm right behind you!" Zahra shouted.

Zahra could not seem to budge the frozen Laura so she let out a barbaric and angry "GO!" as she lifted herself to her mangled legs.

Laura jumped back and turned to hobble her way up the stairs.

Father Jolien smiled as Marcus removed the throw weapon from his jacket.

"What the hell are you smiling about?" Marcus sneered.

"I had a conversation with deputy Weiss." Theoren snapped.

"I'm sure I can dismiss anything you said as the ravings an old man about to kill himself."

"I knew he'd tell you that I disclosed my past. Everyone loves juicy gossip. Especially as juicy as a priest and an illegitimate child. How could he not, really. So, when sister Gershan told me that deputy Weiss needed me in a secluded section of the mountain. I knew I'd find you here." Father Jolien smiled.

"Well, if you knew all that, why the hell are you here? " Marcus growled.

"I had that conversation just before I headed up here. I showed up at deputy Weiss door, told him a story about a corrupt sheriff, about infidelity and violence, and graft. Oh, and by the way, he had suspected much of what I revealed already. I told him that I was going to come up here, to this very spot, and that you were going to kill me." The old priest smirked.

"That's it! Like I said; the ranting of a depressed, suicidal, old fool. Upset about the fact his illegitimate daughter was about to be exposed. Now that Heisten is dead, and your little one-legged cohort is about to meet her end, this town can go back to normal." Marcus raised the nine millimeter and aimed it at Father Jolien's head.

"What did you do to them Marcus!?"

"Sorry, in about seven minutes there's going to be a small propane explosion at the Heisten house. You know those crazy scientists are always messing with dangerous things. Zahra and Laura and the good professor are going to be lost in the blaze. " Marcus sneered before cocking the hammer of the 9mm.

"You didn't let me finish!" Father Jolien's facial expression turned dead serious Marcus grimaced as the priest continued.

"I told deputy Weiss that the only way to rid this town of a bastard like you was for him to get his rifle... position himself on the other side of that gorge....... and kill you first." Jolien finished sympathetically.

Marcus never heard the .308 caliber round explode from deputy Weiss's rifle. Nor did he hear the whistle as it cut air for two hundred meters. The round bored through the back of his skull, and out his right eye socket.

Deputy Weiss pulled his eye from the scope and sat back on his calves, draping the rifle across his thighs. He had come up the mountain to humor Theoren, he knew Marcus was dirty but doubted he would resort to murder. As he began watching the two posture and gesticulate in the silent theater that filtered through his rifle scope, he believed it would end as a harmless miscommunication. Deputy Weiss froze when he saw Marcus pull the nine millimeter from his jacket, while his issued thirty eight remained holster. He recognized what the gun was, an untraceable murder weapon. Having never killed a man before, deputy Weiss struggled to hold his site on Marcus and squeeze the trigger. Just as a panicked deputy Weiss was beginning to fear he might not have the mettle to pull the trigger, Marcus raised the gun and cocked it. It was an image that closed any doubt in Weiss's mind. With renewed focus he zeroed in on the base of Marcus' skull, and painfully squeezed off the fatal round.

The old priest had only driven an ATV once before but some how he willed the machine down the mountain to the Heisten villa in record time. Chunks of mossy dirt rooster-tailed from the thick tires, as he tore across the moraine.

In the basement Zahra's barbaric scream juxtaposed her wobbly and crooked stance. Zahra frantically, though slowly, crawled up the stairs. Her legs and hands too damaged to generate much momentum. Reaching the top of the basement stairs the strong smell of propane gas filled the kitchen. Marcus had turned on the all the burners before exiting.

Laura had run to the nearest exit which was the glass patio door to the rear of the house. She had swung the door open wildly and left it open for her Zahra, who had trailed shortly behind her.

Out the door and across the back patio Zahra did not stop her pathetic awkward stumble until she had gotten fifty meters from the door. She turned and dropped to her back in the mossy alpine grass still several meters from Laura who sat nursing her knees, as she beckoned Zahra toward her.

No sooner had she felt safely out of range of the explosives when she heard voice from inside the house.

"Zahra!" Father Jolien called as he ran through the kitchen toward the basement door.

He had raced through the front door, unaware that all who could be saved lay hobbled in the backyard.

"Father!" Zahra screamed.

The priest was already halfway down the basement stairs, and did not hear her cry.

"Father!" again she screamed.

Zahra fought to stand on her knees, and began moving back to the house. Before she could take a second step the house instantly transformed into a giant ball of flying debris smoke and fire. The colossal blast threw Zahra backward several meters as shards of wood and glass pierced her skin.

Epilogue:

Zahra thought she might have the tiny first class cabin to herself as the train whistled a final boarding notice, but an elderly woman had just popped the flimsy accordion door. Zahra moved over to ease her struggle into the little four seat room.

As she settled into her seat she nodded a polite 'thank you' to Zahra for her consideration. Zahra offered the same silent acknowledgement. The woman was dressed in fur lined felt overcoat, with a matching pill box hat. Her age poorly masked by the excessive makeup she had applied. In contrast, Zahra was clad in a simple sweat suit, and had nothing on her face to cover the clusters of tiny scabs produced by the flying debris.

The old woman looked her over with pity in her eyes. She looked, and felt, like hell. Her hand bandaged and mangled, knee braced, an ill fitting replacement prosthetic attached to her stump, and a pair of crutches were propped against the window. Normally, Zahra would have spent the next hour of thought formulating a story in her mind about the old woman's life. Today however, Zahra's inner dialogue only got so far as "she looks important.", before her mind returned her thoughts back to Father Jolien and the machine. After all, the nice coat, the first class ticket, the demur posture, was it important? What did important mean now? Zahra retrieved a portable stereo from her bag, and inserted the earplugs. As had been the case for the final two days of her stay, she wanted to dissuade any attempts at small talk.

Soothing classical strings filled Zahra's ears as she thought about the old priest. She imagined him reaching the device extracting the explosive charge and closing it just before the explosion. He would have had just enough time.... Maybe. It had taken three hours for the fire department to arrive at the remote compound, and by that time the house was lost. The raging fire was no match for what little water they could extract from Heisten's well, and by the time they ran hose and tapped into the ski company's snow blowing water supply, the house was reduced to a giant bon fire. In fact, it had been two days, and the fire still smoldered from the pit of ashes that was the basement of Heisten's villa.

Strangely, and although Zahra would miss him, she felt happy. He was all about 'stepping up' and making a difference and she was sure he had. "He should be proud" Zahra thought.. She imagined the device rising from the ashes like a phoenix.

Zahra's understanding of the world had been ripped apart and rebuilt in the span of four days. She recalled Dr Heisten theory about the universe pulsing in an out over the course of eons, and about his question "why does there need to be a beginning?".

She felt saddest for Heidi and Laura, who could never have any understanding of what Dr Heisten had died for. She imagined they cursed her, as she was one of the bearers of the device that had brought so much destruction to their lives.

The cog train lurched forward out of the Mornel station. She was on her way home.

The crutches helped cover Zahra's trepidation at approaching the airport customs. Her slow steady approach looked normal with their help. Inside, her heart was racing.

Deputy Weiss had told Zahra that he had no legal right to detain her, but requested she stay in Mornel until his investigation was complete. She hoped that she would not be detained now at the airport.

The customs officer flipped though Zahra's passport before asking "Have you enjoyed your stay?"

"It could have been better." Zahra was aware that these officers were like human lie detectors.

The officer looked up from the passport at Zahra's face.

"You've got some cuts there." He noted perusing her face.

"Yeah, flying glass." Zahra responded honestly..

"Had a bit of an accident?" The officer asked.

"Yeah, unfortunately, but I think it all going to work out." Zahra responded with a nervous smile.

The officer considered her for a long moment before handing her passport back under the Plexiglas barrier that separated them.

"I hope you trip home is better." He smiled back.

The flight home was fully booked, and Zahra had a window seat in first class next to another "important" person; briefcase, slicked grey hair, and a designer suit. Again Zahra inserted her "do not disturb" signs into her ears and selected some mellow jazz from the play list.

She peered out at the strobing light beacons as the plane made its final turn onto the runway.

The engines revved and Zahra was pushed back in her chair by the rapid acceleration.

She found she was less nervous about the plane crashing than she usually was. It just seemed crazy to think that she would die in a

264

plane crash. Now, after all she had been through? The plane shuttered as it broke through he cloud cover, then the plane settled into a smooth climb.

Zahra had the overwhelming sensation that she was not finishing a journey but starting one. She pulled the crystal Dr. Heisten had removed from the device from her pocket, as she recalled what had happened that night.

She had sat by the fire light staring at the crystal and examining the strange markings on the back side of the cartridge that held it. It appeared to be a product label written in some alien language. There appeared to be a rectangular logo in the corner of the label. It was then she decided that Dr. Heisten made sense. She had accepted his theory on the device's origin and intent.

She had entered the basement lab that night not entirely sure what she was going to do. She approached the device holding the tiny transmitter in her fingers as she pondered the possibilities. The flashing icon that showed the device closing seemed to beckon her.

Zahra looked out the plane's tiny oval window as it pitched to the side adjusting it course. Zahra's window now angled up directly at the near moon Aratus and its more distant brother Galios. Zahra smiled as she was reminded of how much she loved this time of year, when the twin moons shared the same night sky. She suddenly noticed she was gently rubbing her belly, and that too made her smile.

It was a beautiful world, and in nine months she would be showing it to someone very special.

C   G

A   T

HTTP://onebegin.com/

Special Thanks:

My entire loving family
Lou Starticen
Carl Lauricella
Don Hine
Fred Creavin
Pete Johnson
Andrew Rodgers
Duncan
&
Dr Lisa M Fustomie

1241207

Made in the USA